Vellichor

By Dawn Napier

Ink Smith Publishing

www.ink-smith.com

ISBN: 978-1-947578-32-6

Ink Smith Publishing
P.O. Box 361
Lakehurst, NJ 08733

Dedicated to the owner and denizens of This Old Book in Grayslake. I haven't gotten lost in there yet, but I keep trying.

Chapter One

Closing time. Helene sighed, breathing deeply of the early night and the smell of old books. She loved her old shop, and she loved most of the customers, but towards the end of the day hers became the exasperated love of an overworked mother. Her stomach rumbled, and she fancied she could already smell the mashed potatoes and gravy she'd prepared for her dinner that morning. All she had to do was pop her plate in the microwave, and dinner was served.

As she shut down the register and turned off her computer monitor, the smell of old books grew stronger. That smell was always present, of course: old paper, ink, and dry dust. The perfume of the ages. But now it was getting stronger, almost cloying. Like a lady's perfume. Helene coughed, and her exasperation tightened into frustration. A sudden surge of that particular perfume always meant a manifestation.

No mashed potatoes for her just yet. "What do you want, Francine?" she asked the air.

The dead woman materialized at Helene's left elbow. There was a stack of 19th-century classics on the table there, but Francine didn't notice. "I'm sorry to bother you, Mrs. Rowe," she said, brushing at her long skirts. "I know you need to get home to your family."

Helene rolled her eyes. Bitch. Francine knew perfectly well that Helene was unmarried and had no children. Although she did need to get home to feed

Nibbles, her geriatric guinea pig. The old girl could barely move these days, but she'd still squeal like a pretty girl in a Hitchcock flick if dinner was late.

In the stories, Helene mused, ghosts were either murderous or tragic. *I've never read a ghost story in which the unquiet spirit was merely obnoxious.*

"What do you want?" she repeated. She tried to say it kindly. It couldn't be easy, being trapped in the world of the living and surrounded by books but unable to pick up a single one to read. *Water water everywhere, and not a drop to drink.*

"I'm sorry to bother you," Francine repeated. She tugged at her ghostly beehive hairdo and patted her cheeks as though checking her makeup. "But— it's out again."

"Which one?"

"It."

God damn it.

Helene's stomach rumbled. But dinner definitely had to wait. It wasn't safe to just let that thing wander around the shop. Some customer must have scuffed the lines of protection Helene had put in place around the shelf.

Ghosts were insubstantial, made mostly of memories and wishes. Francine could annoy Helene from dawn until dusk, but she couldn't actually hurt her.

But not everything that existed here at Enchanted Ink was a ghost. There were other things, too.

Helene hunkered down behind the counter. Behind the cheap .22 rifle that she'd been promising herself for years that she'd eventually replace with a proper shotgun, there was a small plastic case filled with a different sort of protection. Helene selected the plastic bottle of holy water and the sifter of cinnamon and mentally girded her loins.

"You can send it back again, can't you?" Francine asked, as she always did. She sounded like a small child.

"Yes." Helene took a deep breath. Her heart was picking up into that familiar gallop, and she felt her skin going cold and prickly. This wasn't the first time she'd done this, but her body reacted the same way every time. It was some ancient instinct, she thought: the animal's natural aversion to predators.

And whatever else this thing was, it was a predator. Helene had proof of that.

She stalked swiftly toward the back of the shop, to the long row of books labeled Science Fiction, Fantasy, Horror. And there it was.

The boogeyman looked up from the book it was perusing. "Hello, Helene," it hissed. Its black robes flowed around its shrunken body like a river.

"Get back in your book," she said woodenly. "You don't belong out here."

"Christopher says hello." The gaunt, skeletal face drew closer, needle-sharp teeth grinning. "He misses you. He wants you to join him." A long, long finger reached for her face.

"I said get back!" Helene screamed, and she flung the holy water into the monster's face. It hissed and withdrew, but Helene heard a note of amusement under its pain.

Her heart thudded with fear and psychic agony. Hearing Christopher's name in that filthy thing's voice hurt like a razorblade between her ribs.

"By the power of all the forces of good, I command thee, foul spirit." She sprinkled holy water onto the floor in front of her, pushing the boogeyman back toward the shelf. It retreated slowly, grinning the whole time.

"In Jesus's name, I command thee. In the name of the Earth Mother and Sky Father, I command thee. In the name of Ra and Isis, I command thee. Return to your own world, and never return." She flung the bottle at the boogeyman, striking the flowing black shroud. It emitted a hiss like a teakettle, and it shrank away into the stack of books. The black shroud trickled away like water, draining into a large leather tome entitled *Beasts From Beyond: A Tribute to the Masters of Horror*.

Helene picked up the half-empty bottle and capped it, then she sprinkled cinnamon in a wide swath on the floor in front of the shelf. As she'd suspected, the line of salt across the base of the shelf had been disturbed. She would have to reinforce all of her barriers before going home. Fortunately, she'd lost her appetite for dinner.

Being reminded of Christopher did that every time.

"Thanks, Helene," said a young man with enormous muscles encased in a bizarre silver suit. The helmet under his arm looked like a fish bowl with a TV antenna attached. He looked down at the book that the boogeyman had dropped. His face was pale and beaded with sweat. "I hate when he touches my book. I always feel like he could... you know. Like Christopher."

Helene picked up *Voyage Beyond the Stars*. The blaster-wielding hero on the cover was identical to the pale young man next to her, minus the expression of panicky relief.

"He doesn't usually attack the books," she said as she shelved Voyage. "He prefers living souls."

The muscular man opened his mouth to speak, then closed it again. He looked like he wanted to tell her something but was looking for the right words. Helene turned away. Roger always got that look when she mentioned Christopher.

"When was the last time he fed on a living soul?" asked a dour Englishman in a deerstalker cap. He gave Roger a scornful look. "You're starving him, and he's getting desperate."

"She should burn his book," grumbled Roger. "That's what I would do."

"Even if it meant losing her forever?" Helene asked, taking his book out again and showing him the well-endowed blonde simpering on the back cover.

Captain Roger Starr lowered his eyes. Of course not. He would come up with a dangerous but ingenious plan to rescue her, *then* burn the book. It was how his character was written.

"Christopher isn't dead." She put *Voyage* back on the shelf and turned away. "I will find a way to get him out of there. And I promise I'll keep you all safe from the monster until I figure out how."

Francine still stood by the register, and she followed Helene into the back office where she kept her bulk boxes of salt. She fluttered nervously as Helene selected a box and started back toward the horror section. She'd reinforce those lines first, then do the rest of the store. She was going to be late taking her medication, but since she hadn't been to

5

see Dr. Clark in over a year, she didn't have anyone to answer to. It was easier on her stomach to take right before bedtime anyway.

Finally Francine blurted, "Are you sure Christopher's still alive?"

Helene stopped and turned back to the ghost, who backed up and started fussing with her hair.

"I mean, do you have any proof? Maybe the boogeyman is only teasing you, or lying so you won't kill him."

Helene tried not to feel angry. It was a legitimate question, one that she'd asked herself plenty of times. She spoke slowly and carefully to the dead woman.

"I can't take the chance. If I burn that book, Christopher dies. Or worse, trapped in that world forever. That Lovecraftian world with those monsters, and the mad stars... I can't take the chance."

That wasn't the full truth, but Helene was not about to confide in Francine about the dreams she had. Dreams where Christopher came to her and held her, whispering in her ear that he'd found a way to slip through and they had just a moment together before the opening closed and he was pulled back. Back into the world of the dead.

Francine nodded sadly. "Hope is a beautiful thing. Beautiful and terrible."

Helene had to agree.

Chapter Two

"Do you accept donations?" the older man asked. He drummed his thick fingers on the counter, next to the cardboard box he'd sat down in front of her.

Helene fancied she could see her own face in the old guy's enormous blue eyes. He was a big fellow, burly and broad-shouldered, with thinning ginger hair on top. He looked like a retired wrestler or body builder. "We take gently used books in exchange for store credit," she said. "But it depends on what kind of book it is, the condition, how old…"

"I don't need store credit," he interrupted. He sounded hurried, almost out of breath. "Can't hardly read anymore anyway. Just take the books." He slapped the box with the palm of his hand. "I don't have time to read. I don't even have time to be here. Time is very short."

"I understand." Helene glanced into the bag. Mostly trade paperbacks, but Helene saw at least two hardcovers that were probably worth a few dollars. "Are you sure you don't want me to look at these and let you know? You can still buy books for other people. Christmas is coming up."

But he was already heading for the door. "Just keep what you can use and toss out the rest," he called over his shoulder. "I've got to get over to the doctor's down the street."

Helene frowned after the jingling, swinging door. Dr. Dixon's office had been closed for over five years. Had someone else taken over?

****

There were thirteen books in all, most of them the sort of cheap paperbacks found in thrift stores and library sales for a quarter each. A few gothic horrors about sex and revenge, three hardboiled mysteries, a couple of political thrillers, and a romance. Helene discarded the romance right away. It was badly mangled, and she already had three copies of the same novel on the shelf. The others went into her "maybe" pile.

Then she picked up her first hardcover. It was an early edition of a popular horror novel, and Helene frowned at it. She didn't like adding too many horrors to the shop, even though most of the characters were harmless and wanted only to sleep. She hadn't anticipated the blind, eager greed of the boogeyman, and she didn't want to get caught unawares again. But it was a pretty valuable edition, and if she priced it just right it would go quickly. The monster inside had very specific taste anyway, if Helene remembered correctly from the movie. It was unlikely to start trouble in an old book store.

The other hardback... Helene touched it, and she pulled her hand back. Could it be?

She picked up the book and ran her fingers over the raised letters printed on the cover. No dust jacket. That didn't take away from its value, if this was the book she was thinking of. It was. It was the book she'd been looking for. The one she'd unconsciously hoped to find when she'd first inherited the shop.

Vellichor

Imprisonment of Hope by Diana Druid.

And it was a first edition.

Helene wished that she had the old gentleman's contact information. She wanted to thank him for his donation. She wanted to buy him a steak and a beer. And possibly a lap dance.

Imprisonment of Hope was a fantasy novel Helene had read when she was thirteen. It was the first real "grown-up" book she'd ever read, and it had cemented her love of reading and fantasy forever. She'd once wanted to be a writer when she grew up, had even written a few short stories. One of them had been published in an anthology of horror stories, but that had been the last story she'd written. Real life had gotten in the way: college, friends, and that nasty bout of sickness that she was still recovering from. She didn't miss it, mostly.

Helene opened it up and put the page to her face. She sniffed deeply, inhaling the ancient perfume of dust and ink.

This one wasn't going on the shelf. It was coming home with her.

"Wot you got there, mum?" asked a filthy little boy in an oversized men's coat and rubber galoshes. His lilting cockney accent always sounded a bit phony to Helene, possibly because she heard it mocked on British television so frequently.

"New book, Davey," she said, holding it up.

"Wot's it about then?" Davey leaned on the counter, trying to get a closer look.

Helene wished she understood more about the paranormal. They stood on the floor, leaned on the walls, but they couldn't pick up anything. Couldn't open a book or pour a glass of wine. It sounded like hell to her. She wouldn't be able to stand living in a book shop and unable to read. But maybe they didn't miss it, since their lives were literally a storybook.

The boogeyman could pick up books, Helene remembered. But the boogeyman was different. He did all sorts of things that the others didn't, like eat mortal boyfriends.

"It's about a dragon that takes over a kingdom," she explained to the urchin.

"Cor! Wot a dragon want with a kingdom? Gonna eat everyone?"

Helene laughed. "Would you like me to read it to you?" she asked.

"I sure wish ye would, mum." Behind Davey, a handful of other children materialized, and they gathered in close around her.

Well, why not. It was a book for adults, but there wasn't anything too disturbing. She could skim over the sex scenes without interrupting the flow of the story, and she doubted that the vicious Dragon King would be half as frightening as what had happened in Davey's own book. Victorian London was no place for the faint of heart.

And if the Dragon King tried to materialize here, Helene still had plenty of salt and cinnamon handy. Salt, cinnamon, and silver worked on any evil manifestation regardless of its mythology. Reading the book aloud should be safe enough.

She took the book to the back office, settled down in a chair, and began to read. After four pages she discovered that it was just as well the old man hadn't charged her anything for the book. *Imprisonment of Hope* had been defaced.

Vellichor

At least it was easy to ignore. Beginning on page three, there was a question mark in the margin of each page. Just a big blue swirl of ink, as though the previous reader had come across something confusing. On page ten there were two question marks.

How obnoxious. Helene frowned at the book. It was one thing to damage one's own property. But to deface a book and then turn it over to someone else? It was beyond rude. Page twelve had two question marks again. Page thirteen had two questions and an exclamation point. What did that even mean? If the previous owner hadn't understood the story, why not just look up a synopsis on the Internet?

Though, Helene remembered, she had never succeeded in finding a synopsis or any information at all about *Imprisonment of Hope*. Diana Druid must have been a one-off writer like Harper Lee, or a throwaway pen name. She had no history and no bibliography anywhere on the Internet.

But still. Use a notebook for writing down questions as you read, Helene thought irritably. This is a first edition for Christ's sake! Have some respect!

At least she hadn't paid anything for it. That was something. But the nerve of some people, assuming that the rest of the world was dying to know what they thought.

"Are you still reading, mum?" Davey asked.

"I think I'll take a break, actually." Helene hadn't been to the front of the store in a while. The door chime would jingle when a customer walked in, but she still had some minor housekeeping chores to complete before she could close for the day.

"Will ye read more later?" a smaller boy asked. His eyes reminded Helene of those terrible commercials for animal rescues and shelters, the ones with the starving puppies in every frame.

"Of course, Ollie," she said with as maternal a smile as she could muster. Then she put a bookmark in *Imprisonment of Hope* and went up front to spend some time in the real world.

****

"Real world" was a subjective term in Helene's book shop. Two women dressed in 60s hippie garb wandered aimlessly through the romance section, and a large-breasted purple woman lingered in science fiction. Helene knew that they weren't real, because her door had never chimed. And they weren't dead, because they hadn't even noticed her. The real dead people in Enchanted Ink always saw Helene the moment she entered their perceptive range. Usually they stared at her with a hungry sort of expression, one that was more sad than frightening.

The characters weren't looking at the books. That was always the first thing Helene noticed about them. They just wandered around, staring vacantly like lost children.

She cleared her throat. "Can I help you?"

One of the hippies turned to her. "Do you know where we are?" she asked. There were puffy white feathers on leather thongs clipped in her long black hair. "My friend and I are hitchhiking to California, and I think we got lost. We're looking for a place to eat."

Helene knew who they were. They were part of a box of memoir-style chick lit and Westerns someone had inherited from a friend who had moved away. Helene had skimmed a few of them. These were the protagonists of *Journey Across America*, the saga of a couple of college students who ran away from it all after one had been date raped at a party. Helene had read online that the book was only about half true, but it had to be less than that. Real people never manifested as characters in the shop, only people from fiction.

A pity that the nonfiction books never spawned. So many people wandered around her shop in desperate need of therapy. Her psychology section would come in handy, all but Freud, of course. Fuck that victim blaming dick. She saw a therapist a few times a year, but she couldn't afford regular visits. And of course she couldn't tell Dr. Clark everything that was going on in her life, so there wasn't really a lot of point in going.

Helene never knew how to explain the situation to new arrivals, but she did her best. "You're in the real world now. Sort of. You came out of a book. That one." She pointed to *Journey*, prominently displayed in New Arrivals, right next to Romance. "Here in Enchanted Ink, some of the fictional stories come to life and… hang out, I guess."

The black-haired girl peered at it. "But we're real," she objected. "I know we are. It really happened. That—that couldn't have been made up."

"Maybe it's a fictionalized account based on true events," Helene said. She didn't want to come out and say, 'Your author must be a lying sack.' "Most memoirs are only about half the truth. People dress up their stories to make them more interesting."

The other girl spoke up. "I really was raped," she said softly. "I can still—it was real."

"I'm sorry," Helene said gently. "I'm sure it was very real. Here in my shop you'll probably find people to talk to, people who can listen and help you heal."

"That's why we quit school and took off," the black-haired girl said. "Nobody would listen. It was a professor."

The two drew closer together, holding hands in a sort of silent communion. Helene felt like an intruder, so she moved on to the purple woman.

"Are you all right?" she asked. The purple woman was staring down at her own body as though she'd never seen it before.

"I look like a monster," she said. She spoke with an odd accent, Germanic but with rolling Rs. "Why are my breasts so large?"

How odd. Helene had never encountered such self-awareness before. Normally characters behaved the way they'd been written. This one, by the look of her, ought to be a vapid set piece. In lieu of clothing her body was covered in tiny iridescent scales.

"I'm a reptile," the woman went on. "Why do I even have breasts? Breasts are mammary glands; reptiles never have them."

Apparently there were some leaps of logic that even a science fiction character couldn't accept. "I can't help you with that," Helene said. "I'm about to put in a movie. Do you want to watch it?"

"What's a movie?"

"Something we do here to take our minds off our troubles." And keep everyone busy so that Helene could get some actual work done.

Vellichor

She got a real live customer just as she finished setting up the DVD player and turning on a coming-of-age romantic comedy that she thought the hippies would enjoy. The young man snorted when he saw the opening credits. "Showing a movie in a book store?" he asked. "Shouldn't you be promoting, you know, books?"

"Shouldn't you be shopping for skinny jeans?" she responded. Paying customer or no, she wasn't going to take any snark from a kid in high school.

His eyebrows went up. "Touché. Where do you keep the classics? I need something old but easy for lit."

She led him to the appropriate shelf. He took no notice of the various characters in their period costumes stepping out of the shelf and hurrying to the TV screen. Almost nobody saw them but her.

Which brought up the usual question: was she delusional? Maybe none of this was happening. She'd always been an imaginative child, making up stories and pretend characters to help her deal with bullying and loneliness. As a child she'd spent many happy afternoons here, sheltered from reality by books and her friendly aunt. It wasn't out of the question that she could have created all of this in her own head.

But it didn't make sense. She'd been coming here for years, but she hadn't started seeing the characters until she'd inherited the shop. If she was going to start hallucinating, the time to start would have been when she got deathly ill, when she was nineteen.

She stuffed the question back into the locked safe where she kept all her uncomfortable questions and told the teenager, "For old but easy I recommend *1984*, *Brave New World*, or *A Separate Peace*. *1984* is especially good if you spend a lot of time on the Internet talking politics. Everyone likes the phrase 'thought police,' but you'll be the smart guy who actually knows what it means."

"Thanks, ma'am." And the kid actually looked halfway respectful as he paid for *1984* and left.

She shelved a few new books as the movie concluded, and as expected the hippies enjoyed it. They were chatting in bright, cheerful voices as they wandered away back to Memoirs and Literature, and Helene hoped their good spirits would see them through to the end of their book. She hadn't read it from cover to cover, so she had no idea if their ending was a happy one or not. But either way, they deserved a reprieve after what they'd been through.

It was near closing time, and Helene was having visions of chicken salad dancing in her head. So of course that was the exact moment a couple of dirty-faced waifs appeared at her elbow.

"You gonna read more of that book, then?" Ollie asked.

"Just a few pages," Helene sighed. "I want to go home and have dinner."

"We ain't had no dinner in years," Ollie said mournfully. "Nobody reads Dickens anymore."

"All right, stop with the guilt." Ollie grinned, and Helene rolled her eyes. "Let me find that book, and I'll read another chapter."

The Dragon King had captured the Sacred Gem, a relic that belonged only to the rightful ruler of the Walled Kingdom. The gem, Helene already knew, was actually a fragment of unicorn horn.

Vellichor

Unicorns had disappeared from the Walled Kingdom centuries before, when the historical King Jasper had first erected the walls around his kingdom to keep evil wizards from slipping across. Now the Sacred Gem was the symbol of hope for the kingdom, and the witch-seductress Meg had joined forces with the last surviving member of the royal family to retrieve it. Slipping back into the fairytale world of her childhood was like sliding into a warm, comfortable bath. Dinner was forgotten after three pages, and Helene feasted on the familiar words.

She was jarred out of the story when she found more words scribbled in the margins. They made even less sense than the punctuation.

What happened? one read.

What does this mean?

Who are you?

The story was self-explanatory. Why had someone scribbled this nonsense in her new book?

Well, it wasn't a new book. And it wasn't hers. But the principle remained.

Idly, Helene flipped back to the pages where she'd seen the question marks earlier. Then she almost dropped the book.

The marks were gone. In their place were words, scribbled in a long, elaborate scrawl.

What happened?

What does this mean?

Who are you?

"Can you hear me?" Helene asked quietly. She had no idea who or what she was talking to, but six months of dealing with completely random phenomena had desensitized her to the inherent weirdness of talking to a book.

There was no response, of course. It was just a book. She flipped back to the page she had been reading and saw more scribbles in the margins.

Yes, I can hear you. Who are you?

Helene dropped the book. She'd come to accept a great many things since inheriting Enchanted Ink from her aunt, but this was something else.

Was it another character who couldn't manifest for some reason? Or maybe it was a true ghost, like Francine. Or maybe there was a demon trapped in there, imprisoned by arcane magic. Maybe it was the soul of the book's previous owner.

There was a simple way to find out. "I'm Helene. What's your name?"

Then she turned the page.

Helene? It's Christopher! It's me, Christopher!

Helene let out a little whimper and clutched the book to her chest. "Christopher," she whispered. "Are you alive? Are you all right?" She turned the page and read.

I'm all right. It's dark in here. A little creepy. Please keep reading. Your voice pushes the darkness away.

"I don't have time to read now! I have to get you out of there."

Flip.

If you finish reading the book, I'll be able to come through. It's how the spell works.

"All right." Christopher was here, in her hands. He was coming back to her. She raised her voice a trifle. "Who else wants to gather round for story hour? Looks like I'm pulling an all-nighter."

Almost everyone did. Suddenly the shop was crowded with faces of all colors, ages, and species. A pair of flopping tentacles rolled out of nowhere. Almost everyone liked listening to stories. It was a nice change of pace from their own.

Helene sat back in her easy chair, opened a bottle of water from the mini-fridge, and began to read.

The notes disappeared when she started reading, and the pages that followed were clean and perfect. This helped her concentrate on the book and forget everything else, including her scratchy throat.

But behind the wicked doings of the Dragon King and the desperate struggle of the Great Rebellion, Christopher lingered in her mind. He was going to be free at last. This must be one of the weak spots he'd told her about, a thin patch of reality where he could push through to the other side. She'd known that he would find a way back to her. Christopher had always found a way to do whatever he wanted.

Deep into the night she read to her literally breathless audience. Nobody moved or shifted, coughed or fidgeted. It was like reading to an enormous mural.

Except one. Out of the corner of her eye Helene saw Ollie dancing from foot to foot. He acted like he needed to go to the bathroom, but of course book characters never went to the bathroom unless it was essential to the plot.

Finally she asked, "Ollie, what's the matter?"

He dropped his eyes. "Don't know, mum. Just feel twitchy. Like a storm's coming."

Maybe Christopher was close to getting through. But that shouldn't frighten the boy. He'd never seemed afraid of Christopher while he was in the shop. "How are our new friends getting along? Are they settling in on their shelves?"

Ollie shrugged. "We're all fine out here. The storm's comin' from you."

Helene frowned and looked down at the book in her hands. He had to mean *Imprisonment of Hope*. Was there something else in there near Christopher, a demon or monster like the boogeyman, trying to keep him away? There were witches and monsters a-plenty in there, not to mention the Dragon King himself.

She turned the page uneasily. She wondered if she should ask Christopher.

I love you Helene was written in the margin.

"I love you too, Chris," she said slowly. "Are you okay in there?"

Flip. Getting better all the time. I'm coming closer to you. Remember the beach?

"Yes. I told you to put on sunscreen, but you wanted to tan."

Flip. And I got so red I could barely stand to be touched that night.

"Yes."

Flip. But you found a few places where I wasn't sunburned, didn't you?

Helene giggled. "Yes, I did."

Flip. I can't wait to touch you again.

"Me too." Helene glanced at Ollie. "Hon, if you're bothered why don't you go back to your book? I've only got a few chapters left."

Ollie scowled and looked down. "Wanna know how it ends," he muttered.

"Then please settle down and let me finish." Helene opened another bottle of water and resumed reading.

An hour or so later, Helene had to stop again. Now more of her audience was fidgeting and looking around. Captain Roger Starr, he of the silver space suit, was looking up at the ceiling as though expecting something to fall from there.

Francine cleared her throat and tapped a scrap of paper on the table next to her chair. Helene frowned and picked it up.

Pickles, turkey, rye bread, mayo, beer. Lots of beer. Chips. Apples or grapes or some shit.

It was a shopping list that Christopher had written out and somehow left lying around here. Where had Francine found this? And how had she brought it here to set on Helene's table?

And why did it even matter? So Christopher sort of sucked at picking out fruit, oh well.

Francine cleared her throat again and nodded at the book in Helene's hands. She tapped the side of her nose.

"Christopher?" Helene said.

Flip. Yes, baby doll? Are you still reading? You're almost at the good part.

She was; she remembered how it ended. The Dragon King would destroy the Rebellion, burning the headquarters in a violent firestorm that would turn the mountains to ash and rubble. The book ended on a tragic note, with the Dragon King roaring his triumph at the skies, and the heroes holding each other as they expired.

The epilogue was more hopeful, implying that a survivor had been born in a faraway village who would eventually grow up to challenge the King and take back the country. But as far as Helene knew, that sequel had never been written. Diana Druid had disappeared off the face of the earth after *Imprisonment of Hope*. Helene had never even found the book on any fantasy wiki sites.

But never mind. Helene read Christopher's shopping list, and the words scribbled in the margins of the book. And she saw what Francine wanted her to see.

The handwriting was nothing alike.

Francine nodded meaningfully.

"I need to take a break," Helene said. "My throat hurts."

Please hurry back. I miss you.

Francine closed the book and put it down. She went to her back office and looked around for her canister of salt. On her desk was a pad of sticky notes.

Written on the top note was, *Helene? Are you there?*

She pulled off the note and crumpled it up. The next note read, Please pick up my book again. I miss you so much. I love you, Leenie.

Helene's heart hurt. Maybe it really was Christopher. How else would he know to use that pet name?

She found the salt canister and picked it up. If it was Christopher, this would do him no harm and might get him out faster.

She carried the salt back to the chair behind her computer and sat down. "All right, Christopher," she said. "I'm ready to read some more."

She set the canister down and opened the book.

I'm so glad. I want you so bad, Leenie.

That was classic Christopher. Whenever he felt sentimental, he sounded like a bad romance novel. Helene desperately wanted to be wrong about this.

"The Dragon King reared his head back and roared a challenge to the sky."

As she read, Helene reached for the salt. Or she tried to. She couldn't take her hand off the book.

"Absinthe drew her sword, fearing desperately that this battle would be her last. But she couldn't run away. She had to kill the Dragon King or die in the attempt."

Stop reading, she thought. Close your mouth, shut your yap, close the book, just stop reading and grab that fucking salt!

She couldn't stop either. She tried to bite her tongue, but it just went on flapping, shaping the words of the book that possessed her. Her lips moved numbly, as though they belonged to someone else. And in a way, they did. Helene could feel the dark presence behind the book now, pressing into her head and forcing the words out of her mouth.

How had she believed that it was Christopher? She must have been stupid or desperate, or both. This was something real, something evil, with the power to read her thoughts and mine her memories for useful information to use against her.

"The humans were doomed, their burned bodies flying through the air to die in a bloody heap.

The Walled Kingdom had become a killing pen for the Dragon King. But still they pressed on…"

And so Helene pressed on, fighting the compulsion even as it pressed down on her hands and mouth. She could feel the heaviness the others had spoken of. It felt like an enormous weight, a pressure in the air, as though something huge and heavy were about to collapse on them.

The children were long gone. She had no idea when they had disappeared. She tried to think of when she'd last seen them, but her brain felt fuzzy and blank. All she could think of was the book, and the darkness behind the pages.

"A few fled, running from the fires like rats deserting a burning barn. The Dragon King licked his chops. Fear made the meat so tender."

Helene was shaking with fear as she continued to read. She didn't know what was about to happen, what vile creature was about to erupt out of the book. Maybe it was the Dragon King himself. What would happen to the shop? The books?

Burning a book was the only guaranteed way to kill a character here at Enchanted Ink. And they did not die easily.

Davy. Ollie. The British detective, the hitchhiking hippie girls. The multitudes of people and creatures who came and went like ships in the night. They would all be destroyed, and it was her fault. Why had she just assumed that the writing in the book belonged to Christopher? He had never defaced a book in his life.

She was on the last page of the epilogue. The ink was blurred and starting to run, but she could still make out the words. More was the pity.

Vellichor

"And as the baby gurgled up at the spinning toy, the young peasant woman thought that—"

And just like that, the book was gone. "Hey!" Helene shouted in spite of herself. "I was reading that!"

The grey-haired woman held the book in a pair of iron tongs that looked like something one would use to maintain a fireplace. "Yes, and it looks like I got here just in time. Grab that salt, miss."

Helene was too frazzled to do anything but obey. The older woman wore wire-rimmed glasses and a mishmash of plaid and paisley that would look at home on a 60s love child. Which, Helene supposed, this woman was the right age to be. She opened up the salt canister, and the hippie grabbed it.

"Stand back," she warned, and Helene was happy to comply. Then the hippie dropped the book, uttered some sort of nonsense that sounded like conversational Latin, and dumped the entire canister of salt over it.

The book exploded, and Helene screamed. *My book!* she thought hysterically, but the hippie held her hands over the conflagration and uttered more gibberish. The fire died down almost instantly, and within minutes there was nothing left but a small pile of ash in the middle of a scorched carpet.

No, that wasn't true. Helene looked down at the pile of ash, and she felt her eyes go wide. The book was scorched but intact. Probably still readable, though Helene was afraid to find out.

"So it's come to this," the old woman said. She picked up the book with thumb and forefinger and dropped it onto the counter. "The good news is, my journey is at an end. The bad news is... apparently this is going to be harder to do than I thought."

"Sorry, who are you?" Helene blinked at the woman.

"I'm not normally one for burning books, but I don't think it counts when it's your own, does it? Good evening. I am Diane Landon. Diana Druid to you."

Chapter Three

(Six Months Earlier)

The rain thumped down on the green canvas awning, creating a wall of water that protected the store from potential customers like a force field.

"Nobody likes to buy books in the rain," Christopher complained.

"I know." Helene didn't lock up from her book. He'd been parroting the same line all morning.

But then he finally took it to the next level. "You should close early," he said brightly, as though the thought had just occurred to him. "We can go home, make some popcorn, put in a movie. It's the perfect day for it."

"You can go if you want to," Helene said. She closed the book, leaving a finger between the pages to mark her place. "I told you earlier that I'm just going to read all day. If you want to go do something else, have at it."

"No, I'll stay." Christopher dropped his skinny butt into a nearby chair and picked up a random book. It was one of the books about paganism that Helene had just finished. "You need me to keep you company."

Then please shut up, Helene thought as loudly as she could. *You don't have to stay here. I don't need your help. Customers aren't exactly beating down the door. So go if you want to go, but don't choose to stay and then bitch the whole time. Jesus.*

She re-opened the book, and she had just found her place again when he asked, "What are you reading, anyway? That doesn't look like the stuff you usually read."

Dear, sweet baby, Jesus, help me not to hurt this man. She closed the book again. "They're books my aunt left sitting on the counter. I figured they were important."

"Are you sure she didn't just leave them there by mistake?"

Help me. "There was a note with my name on it sitting on top of the stack."

"What did the note say?"

"Just my name."

After a few minutes of silence, Helene decided it was safe to open the book again. Christopher appeared to have finally gotten the hint, because he got up to wander the stacks toward the back of the used book store his girlfriend had inherited.

Helene wasn't sure why Aunt Sarah had left these particular books sitting out, with her first and last name definitively drawn in huge block letters on a bright pink sticky note. She didn't know this any more than why she'd left the shop to her in the first place. Sarah's own daughter Tess had gotten all the cash and the bit of land up north, but the shop had been left to Helene. She'd been glad to have it; she'd spent a good part of her late adolescence here, browsing the books and doing her homework in the quiet back office. Tess had been more popular, more fond of noise and excitement. Maybe that's all it was.

Vellichor

But the books were interesting. Old-fashioned witch lore mostly, with spells for healing, relaxation, and various tips and tricks for keeping demons and ghoulies and long-legged beasties out of one's living space. Most of these last seemed to indicate that Helene needed to spruce up her spice rack. She didn't think any monstrosities from the abyss would be repelled by ten-year-old oregano or musty cloves.

She sensed that someone was standing in front of her. The door chime hadn't rung, so it must be Christopher, back with some new torment.

Helene was startled to see a young man in a torn grey T-shirt standing in front of her. There was a smear of blood on his upper lip, as though he had recently had a nosebleed. She smelled smoke, but not cigarette smoke. Not weed smoke either. What was burning?

"Can I help you?" she asked slowly. The rain thudded down outside. It was very warm and sticky in here. She hadn't needed to turn on the air conditioning yet; it was still spring. But today, she thought maybe she should. He wasn't even wet.

He stared at a spot behind her head and didn't seem to hear her. "Can I help you?" she repeated. He was probably a college student coming to ask if she had the newest YA dystopian fantasy (she usually didn't) or an obscure science fiction novel (she usually did.) But there was something odd about him. Maybe she was just surprised by his sudden appearance, or perhaps it was the surreal lighting caused by the rain outside and the burned-out light overhead. But there was something odd about the way he stood in front of her and stared straight past her eyes. He didn't seem high, but he wasn't all there, either.

"Is there something you're looking for?" she asked, a little louder. It would be a fine thing to be spooked by this strange fellow only to find out that he was deaf or had some other special need.

"You," he said, finally looking at her. His eyes were very blue. His face was pale and framed by shaggy black hair. "I need you. It's getting out. And there's someone back there, right next to it."

"What?" The guy was acting like a character from a ghost story. Well, she was surrounded by books. It was the best place to have one. And there had been a few oddities about this shop, things Christopher hadn't believed...

"Your aunt left a few things in the desk under the register. She knew you'd need them. I saw the books she left you."

If this guy was a robber hoping to get her to drop her guard by bending down and looking under the counter, he was sadly mistaken. That was where she kept her .22 pistol. It wasn't much of a gun, but it would do fine against a skinny drink of water like this.

She put a hand on it while she peered into the gloomy dark under the register. Back against the far wall she saw what he was talking about. There was a cardboard salt canister, two smaller canisters of some sort of spice, a Zippo lighter, and a wooden mallet. She nudged the items around and was not surprised to see a thick wooden stake as well.

Where are the silver bullets? she thought. Her aunt had been weirder than she thought.

Vellichor

Next to the mallet was a cardboard box that looked like it had once held shotgun shells. She put a hand inside and felt cold, metal objects like ball bearings. She took one out. It was tarnished, grey, and the size of a cat's-eye marble.

No silver bullets, but slugs or projectiles of some kind. Helene held it in her fist for a moment, enjoying its heft and weight.

Put together with the books Aunt Sarah had left for her, and she was getting an interesting picture of the sort of person her aunt had been. Funny; Helene had known her well enough as a teenager and had never noticed anything out of the ordinary about her. But Helene had had her own problems to deal with.

"Could you please hurry?" the young man said. He leaned over the counter to look down at her, and from this angle it looked like he was leaning through it, as though he and the counter somehow overlapped. "It's been getting stronger, and it's almost out again."

"I'm coming." Helene thought, what the hell, and grabbed the salt and the silver, leaving the .22. If this was a trap, she could still throw the salt in the creepy little man's eyes.

The young man led her to the back of the store. He moved so swiftly and silently that he seemed to float, and Helene felt like a lumbering elephant trying to keep up. She also felt foolish for following him, and for taking him even remotely seriously. But there was an odd little prickle at the back of her neck, the tickle that came when she closed the shop alone and noticed the young men at the bar across the street, watching her. That bar was the reason she'd bought the .22 and taught herself how to shoot it.

Then she heard the scream. It was Christopher.

She bolted past the stranger as though he was made of air, turned the corner, and stopped dead. What she saw was so bizarre that for a crucial moment she couldn't move. She only stared, trying desperately to make sense of what she was seeing.

The closest shelf was labeled Sci-Fi, Fantasy, and Horror. The books were lined up neatly, alphabetized by author, and that was where the rational world ended.

From one of the lower shelves a black, baggy shape stretched. It looked like moving oil, or melting taffy. The shape reached and stretched in midair. It stretched to face her.

A hideous, withered face with dancing blue sparks for eyes and a grey, rotting grin. Helene took a deep, sobbing breath.

Long, grasping claws held Christopher's pale, bleeding body like the legs of a spider.

If that hadn't been horrifying enough, it also looked familiar. Terribly, horribly familiar. Where had Helene seen this horror before? It was like the memory of a childhood dream. The thing in the closet, or under the bed.

But Christopher was still alive. Hurt and terrified, but his mouth still worked and drew breath. One ragged claw had pierced his left ear, and dark blood flowed down his neck in a ragged trickle.

His head flopped, and his rolling eyes caught a glimpse of her, standing there speechless and stupid. He shouted, "Helene, run!"

Vellichor

The Thing looked up at her and hissed. Helene remembered the salt canister, and she opened it slowly.

"Hello there, little lady," it murmured in a lilting, serpentine voice. "I thought well of your aunt."

"My aunt is dead," Helene said clearly. She poured a little salt into her hand and leaned back a little.

"Oh, what a shame. She was a worthy foe. Well, I suppose you'll do. Say goodbye to loverboy."

The creature opened its jaws impossibly wide, gaping teeth like the maw of a snake. The gaping hole of mouth enveloped Christopher's pale face and bleeding head. "No!" Helene screamed. She leaped forward and flung the salt into the creature's face.

It hissed and spat Christopher out, but before Helene could react its flowing black cloak swarmed over his semiconscious body and buried him in darkness. The cloak was so black that Helene could see no folds or shadows in the flowing shroud.

"You *are* worthy," it crooned. "I look forward to our dance. Helene."

"What are you?" Helene shouted.

"Oh, for shame. I know you've heard of me. You more than anyone know exactly what I am." The shadowy creature flowed closer to her, and Helene held up the box of salt. It withdrew and trifle and said, "Everyone has heard of me. I live in children's closets and under their beds. I eat fear."

"The boogeyman," she whispered.

"Clever girl." The boogeyman's withered face widened in a rotten grin. "I remember you, little bookworm. Did you miss me?"

Helene had no recollection of this shadowy nightmare, but she knew that she'd forgotten most of her childhood fears. There had been so many. "Give Christopher back," she said.

"Come and get him!" And with a whirling flourish, the boogeyman swept away, back into the bookshelf.

Helene was alone in the shop.

Chapter Four

Diana Druid drank a bottle of water and ate half of Helene's emergency pretzels before she would say anything of note. "Sorry," she mumbled around a mouthful. "Hungry. Long trip. Took a lot out of me."

"Take all the time you need," Helene said. She thought about Nibbles, who was probably staring out of the bars of her cage as though the universe was conspiring to destroy her spirit. But being a little late for dinner wouldn't kill the fat old thing. She could probably stand to miss a few meals.

"Who's the dead girl?" Diana asked, flicking her gaze over Helene's shoulder. Helene turned and was not surprised to see Francine standing a few feet away, fussing with her beehive as though it had gotten mussed.

"That's Francine," she said. "She came with the shop."

"She's not a character. She's a real person, or she was."

"Yes." Helene glanced back at Diana with surprise. It had taken her weeks to get to know the people here well enough to pick up on the difference between a book character come to life and a real ghost. The book people had a brightness about them that the dead lacked, like psychic neon. Francine's color was faded, her lips and cheeks pale and washed out despite her expertly applied lipstick and blush.

"So what's her story?" Diana shook the empty water bottle, and Helene handed her another one.

"I don't know." Helene repeated, "She came with the shop."

"And you never talked to her? You never asked a dead woman how she came to haunt your property? Or why she's dressed as a Victorian lady even though this building can't be more than fifty years old?"

Helene had honestly never given it a moment's thought. When Francine showed up she normally brought bad news that required immediate action, so Helene had never been in a position to sit and have a casual conversation with her.

"I've had a lot going on lately," she said. "My boyfriend, Christopher—"

"Yes, he was the one who called me. And it looks like I got here just in time. The Dragon King was almost loose."

Helene took a quick breath. "What?"

"Hey, Francine." Diana addressed the specter behind Helene. "Tell us about yourself. How did you die?"

"What did you say about Christopher?" Helene leaned forward.

"Hush." Diana gave Helene a sharp look, and Helene closed her mouth. She needed all the help she could get, and if this Diana person thought that Francine could help, then Helene decided to let her take the lead.

And she was a little curious, now that the subject had come up. The building had been built in the late sixties, but Francine's garb was from at least a hundred years ago. She wouldn't look out of place on the set of Amadeus.

"Yes, Francine," Helene chimed in. "Tell us about yourself. We never get a chance to really talk."

Francine patted her hair one last time and stepped forward. "It was a fire," she said breathlessly. "There were too many people in the apartment, the halls were crowded, everyone was drunk. We never stood a chance. Twenty-six people died."

"That's terrible," Helene said.

"I didn't burn up. I was trampled by the crowd. Someone knocked me down and stepped on me, and there were others after him."

As she spoke, a single drop of blood fell from her nostril and landed on her bodice.

"That's so terrible," Helene repeated. She'd known that Francine was dead of course, but she'd never bothered to wonder how it had happened. Francine had always just been there, a singularly annoying and constant presence. For the last six months Helene had been too preoccupied with Christopher's disappearance to think about anyone else's back story.

"I'm sorry that happened to you," she said, but Francine rolled her eyes.

"Don't feel sorry for me," she said as she patted her hair. Another drop of blood rolled out of her nose, giving her a lopsided Charlie Chaplin mustache. It reminded Helene of the bloody-faced man who had appeared the day Christopher had been taken. He, she had later found out, was another dead person. He rarely showed himself unless something bad was about to happen.

"I may be dead, but at least I got to live first. I didn't spend my life reading moldy books and playing with a rat."

"Nibbles is a guinea pig," Helene snapped.

"You should have seen me at the party that night. My beehive wig took two hours to put together just right, and the bodice made my twins pop out to here."

"I can see what you looked like. You're still wearing the costume, genius."

"The bustle was a mistake. That was why I couldn't run, and I got knocked down. But still—I was a knockout."

"Diana, why are we doing this?" Helene asked in exasperation. Why on earth did this stranger think that Francine had anything worthwhile to say?

"You should listen to the dead more often," Diana chided. "Among the inane babbling you can often find bits of wisdom."

Helene sighed and sat down. She couldn't remember the last time Francine had said anything remotely interesting, let alone useful.

Francine looked vindicated. "So do you want to know why I became a ghost?" she asked. Her tone was challenging, as though she dared Helene to say no.

"I'm on the edge of my seat," Helene said, and Diana frowned at her.

"It's because I met my one true love that night," she said dreamily. "The one I was destined to be with forever. We were supposed to fall in love and get married, except for that stupid fire."

"Was he the same guy who trampled you?"

"No!" Francine stamped her foot, and Helene was surprised when it made a loud thump on the threadbare carpet. Diana sat up a little straighter.

"He was tall and handsome, and he laughed at my jokes and we talked about our childhoods... I don't actually remember what we talked about. I don't remember... But it doesn't matter. We made a ritual that night that was supposed to bind us together forever. The fire—the fire started just after the ritual."

"How did the fire start?" Diana asked.

Francine frowned. "I don't know. I was with him—we were—cuddling. I smelled smoke, and then everyone was pushing, and then I was on the floor, and there were feet on my back. And on my head. Someone fell and slammed their knee into my neck. I think that was when I stopped breathing."

Helene shuddered. She was both introverted by nature and a bit claustrophobic, so she hated crowds as a general rule. Francine's death was just about the worst she could imagine. Except maybe for burning to death.

"I saw him one last time as I lay dying," Francine crooned, staring at the ceiling. "He was standing very close to me, just out of reach in the crowd. He was looking all around, trying to find me. Then the crowd pushed him away, and he was gone. And then—so was I."

"I see." Helene spoke as kindly as she could. "And so you became a ghost because...?"

"My spirit can't rest until I know what became of him." Francine brushed at her nose, sending a blood droplet flying away. It landed on the carpet, soaked in, and disappeared. "I know he's not waiting for me, but I need to know that he's happy, that he moved on and found love with someone else. He's probably married by now. With lots of kids."

"How long ago did you die?"

Francine shrugged. "Thirty years? Maybe? I've lost track. They cleaned up the mess and got all the bodies out, but nobody wanted to move back in. So the owners sold it, and I think it was your aunt who bought it and made it into a book store. Then those other people started showing up."

"Do you want us to find this young man of yours?" Diana asked, sitting forward in her chair. "Maybe it would help you find peace."

"I'd love it if you could." Francine didn't sound optimistic. "No offense, but it's so dreary around here. You can't play any really good movies because of the kids, and I can't even pick up a book to read. I wish I could go to heaven and see my cousin again."

"Your cousin?"

"He fell out of a tree when he was ten. Stayed in a coma for a month before he died. I still remember him lying in bed in my uncle's back bedroom. Like a little prince from a fairy tale."

Diana cocked her head and blinked. Then she shook her head. "I'm sorry. We'll do everything in our power to help you find peace and see your cousin again. Helene, could we go up to your apartment? I'd like to do some research."

She had an Internet connection on her personal computer in the back office, but Helene thought that what Diana was really asking for was privacy. Francine had just given them a lot of information to digest.

There was a back exit behind Helene's office that led to a narrow stairwell and up into her apartment. Diana grinned as Helene led her upstairs and unlocked the second door. "Neat," she said. "Like a secret passageway."

"It was one of the reasons I moved here when my aunt left me the store," Helene said. "My old place was only twenty minutes away, but I just fell in love with the idea of a back door into my own book shop."

Nibbles started wheeking the moment they stepped through the door. She couldn't remember the last time she'd fed the poor thing, though she should still have plenty of water. Normally Nibbles got her dinner at seven o'clock sharp, one hour after closing time. Now it was almost four in the morning, and apparently she wanted Helene to know that she was wasting away to nothing.

"Kitchen's that way," Helene said, pointing. Diana could hardly miss it; the apartment was so small she could see the whole place from any vantage point. "There's a bottle of cheap red on the counter if you want, or there's a few bottles of the good stuff in the cabinet over the sink."

Diana headed into the kitchen while Helene fed her starving, neglected guinea pig. Nibbles purred eagerly as Helene filled her bowl with kibble and added a fistful of hay to her manger. Helene scratched Nibbles' back as the pig knocked her bowl over with her nose and set to work cleaning up the mess.

"Crazy old thing," Helene murmured. Then she went to the kitchen to fortify herself with a glass of Vitamin A, for alcohol.

Diana had already poured them each a fat glass of the red merlot Helene usually finished the work day with. As Helene entered the kitchen, she raised her glass. "To new-found friends," she said.

Nibbles wasn't the only one who hadn't eaten on schedule, so Helene found and opened a box of crackers and a pack of cheese slices. Then she sat down and raised her own glass. "Cheers," she said. Maybe it was the sleep deprivation or the fact that she'd narrowly escaped being soul food for some psychic monster, but she felt downright giddy. Like she could take on the world and wash it down with a glass of wine.

She remembered that she wasn't supposed to take wine with her medication, but she decided it didn't matter. She'd forgotten her evening dose anyway. What the hell, we all have to die of something, she thought.

She drank half the glass in a single gulp, and as the gentle warmth suffused her stomach, she quickly chased it with several crackers and bits of cheese. It wouldn't do to get drunk too quickly and pass out now. Diana had information she needed.

"So how did you find me?" she asked after swallowing. "You said Christopher called you? You showed up in the nick of time, just like in a book."

"It was exactly like something out of a book. My book. I was following it, trying to track it down. I thought I knew where it was: in an old man's attic. But then I lost the trail, and I was casting about for it when I caught a signal from someone on the other side. It was a young man's voice, shouting for help. He sounded frantic, and when I tracked him down I heard your voice, echoing on both sides of the veil.

Vellichor

You were reading the book, and once I'd heard it, it was like following a silver thread. I had to haul ass to get there in time though. You're a fast reader."

"How did you get in the shop? It was locked; we were closed for the night. And I have barriers against magic."

"Yes, but those barriers only work against evil. Your guardians knew I meant well, so they let me in."

"Guardians?"

"Salt, cinnamon, and holy water aren't barriers by themselves. They attract positive energy that in turn attracts beings that feed on the light and hate anything evil. They know me over there. I've done them a few favors."

"I never knew how that worked."

"Well, now you do. But now we need to talk about Francine."

Helene shrugged and ate another cracker. She was embarrassed to admit that she knew so little about the omnipresent spirit inhabiting Helene's personal space. It wasn't that she didn't care, exactly—but it probably appeared that way.

But Diana seemed to understand. "You've had a lot to deal with in the last year," she said. "You probably never gave much thought to Francine, because whenever she's around, there's something else going on. Right?"

"Yeah, I guess." Helene plopped a piece of cheese on top of another cracker. She washed it down with another gulp of wine.

"How many other dead people are there in Enchanted Ink? Do you know?"

"At least three. Francine, a young man who seems to get a lot of nosebleeds, and a little old lady who roams around all night and never talks to anyone. And maybe a baby."

"A baby?"

Helene nodded and finished her wine glass. "I never see it. Just hear it crying sometimes."

"How do you know it's a ghost, if you've never seen it?"

Helene paused with a cracker halfway to her mouth. "I don't know. Just a feeling."

"Well, let's go with that. It's usually good to follow your instincts." Diana refilled Helene's glass and topped off her own.

Helene sighed. "I didn't have very good instincts about that book, though, did I? It sucked me in... I felt like it was going to eat me."

"We'll talk more about that later. Right now let's focus on Francine."

"Oh for heaven's sake, why? Of all the shit I've got going on right now—"

"She's the only dead person in your shop who seems to take an active interest in its goings-on. That makes her interesting to me. And when you've been chasing shadows as long as I have, you learn to trust your gut."

Helene shrugged. "All right. So what do you want to do about her? Find this one true love of hers?"

"We'll start by looking up the fire, and then play it by ear. I think we'll find out more if we don't have a clear objective."

Helene had a laptop computer that she used for online gaming and yelling at strangers on social media. She fired it up and found her favorite search engine. "Type in the building's address and add 'fire,'" Diana instructed unnecessarily.

Just as she was about hit Enter, Diana said, "Do you smell something?"

Helene sniffed. "Just dust and old books."

"Does your apartment normally smell like your shop?"

"Usually it smells like microwaved food and timothy hay. Should I be worried?"

"Helene, help!" Francine screamed.

Helene jumped off the couch, dumping her 800-dollar machine onto the floor. "What the hell are you doing here?"

The dead woman was even paler than usual, almost transparent and wavering like a heat mirage. "Please help, he's here!"

"Something got out." Helene bolted for the door. "I bet it was the fucking boogeyman again."

"Has Francine ever manifested in your apartment before?" Diana followed her down the stairs, pulling something out of her jeans pocket on the way.

"No. I didn't know she could. Nobody's ever left the shop before, except Christopher."

The bloody man who smelled like smoke was standing at the bottom of the stairs. Helene brushed past him as he raised one hand and said, "Oh good, I was looking for you."

But it wasn't the boogeyman this time. It was a black, slimy tentacle rolling and thrashing right in the middle of the main walkway. Which was adjacent to Science Fiction, Fantasy, and Horror.

The tentacle slopped and recoiled all over the cheap flowered carpet, leaving a silvery trail of slime. Helene studied it carefully. The trail wasn't fading when the tentacle moved away. This was one of the monsters that might be a little bit real. Hopefully it wouldn't tear up any of the shelves.

"Salt," Helene said. "I need my salt."

"I've got something that might work," Diana said. She stepped forward and pulled a black pendant from around her neck. It looked like a triangle that glittered in the dim light of the shop. She took it off her neck and held it out to the thrashing black coil of tentacle. It froze when the pendant drew close, and seconds later it whiplashed back into the book like a black snake.

There was still a slimy trail of mucus smeared across the carpet where it had been just a moment before.

"Gross." Helene wrinkled her nose. "If that's real, I'm going to have to clean it up before I open the shop tomorrow."

"How many of these characters are capable of manifesting physically?" Diana asked. She sounded out of breath.

"Just one or two." Helene followed the snail trail back to the shelf, and of course it was that damned book again. The same collection that the boogeyman was from. "I should burn that fucking thing—but I don't want to lose Christopher."

"I understand."

Helene watched Diana tuck the pendant back under her shirt. "What was that?"

"A pendant against demonic possession. I figured it would work against—whatever that thing was."

"An unnamed horror from some Lovecraftian universe. I read the book a long time ago. I guess 'demon' works as well as anything. God I hope that slime dissipates on its own."

Helene went to the front desk, where the mysteriously unburned *Imprisonment of Hope* lay. She reached for it, but Diana grabbed it first.

"Better not touch it," she said. "You've read all but the last line. The Dragon King might be able to get to you again."

Helene was happy to never touch or look at the damn thing again. She looked around the shop and was not surprised to see Francine hovering near New Arrivals, wringing her hands like a fussy old maid.

"How did you make it up to my apartment?" Helene asked. "None of you have ever done that before."

"I don't know." Francine adjusted her bodice and tugged at the sleeves of her costume. "I saw the thing and just got scared. I didn't think about it. I just knew I had to find you."

"Uh-huh." Helene didn't like this. She'd always considered her apartment a sanctuary from all the craziness. Was it really, though, if the creatures from down here could still reach her if they really wanted to?

She didn't want to think about it anymore.

"I'm going home, and I'm going to bed," she announced. "You all can do whatever you want, but I am officially done with this day. So good night, and go to hell."

And with that Helene marched back upstairs and went to bed. She was aware that she'd left a weird hippie witch alone in her bookstore, but she was so tired and pissed off at the world that she didn't care. Her brain and body were completely exhausted.

Chapter Five

Helene slept deeply and blessedly without dreams. At one point a warm presence came and lay beside her, and in her deep state she thought it was Christopher and happily snuggled against him. When she awoke the presence was gone, if it had ever existed.

She lay still for a long time, staring at the cracked ceiling and taking stock of her situation. There were more water stains than she remembered. The roof was leaking again. Mother fuck. As though she didn't have enough problems. Her bed was deep and soft, her pillow slightly musty. She hadn't washed her bedding in a while. That was something she'd done more often with Christopher around; his allergies kept him up all night if the sheets and pillows weren't washed every other day or so. She hoped there were no allergies wherever he was.

She was getting off track. Back to the present. Her mouth was dry, her head slightly achy with the need for coffee. Also a bit achy in the nethers; she hadn't had sex in months. There had been one hookup about two months after Christopher's disappearance, and it had been a disaster. A former coworker from a fast food place, someone she'd thought she could trust to be respectful and discreet. She'd been wrong on both points, plus he'd been a terrible lay. She needed Christopher back.

Downstairs there was a book that somehow resisted being burned. There was a witch who was also an author, an author who had no compunctions about burning that book. Add that to the motley cast of book characters, ghosts, and boogeymen, and she was in for a hell of a day.

From her cage nearby, Nibbles whistled hopefully. Good. Start with something easy. Feed the guinea pig. Helene slowly hauled her aching body out of bed and headed for the kitchen.

There was a leak somewhere in the fridge that she had never gotten around to fixing. The bowl she kept under the leak was full of icy water, so she dumped it into the sink and replaced the bowl before rummaging around for Nibbles' morning ration of romaine lettuce and carrots. The romaine was almost gone; she was down to the icky white parts in the middle. Nibbles wouldn't care. Helene took the veggies back to the bedroom and watched with pleasure as the fat little pig purred and tucked in.

Now for her own breakfast. Helene's stomach roiled; all she really wanted was coffee. She started a pot brewing and opened the cabinets one after another, thinking that there might be raisins or crackers, something mild she could eat without puking. But there was nothing. She hadn't been shopping in weeks.

Fuck it. She'd just have coffee. Skipping one meal wouldn't kill her.

Just as she had finished adding sugar and half and half, there was a knock at her door. The back door, the one that connected directly to the shop downstairs.

"You'd better be human!" she announced as she went to open it. "And alive," she added under her breath. She couldn't deal with ghosts or ghoulies before she'd even taken a sip of coffee.

"As far as I know I am," Diana said from the other side of the door. "Can I come in? That coffee smells wonderful."

Helene couldn't say no to a fellow coffee enthusiast. She opened the door and let the older woman in. Diana went straight to the kitchen and helped herself. It seemed a bit presumptuous to Helene, but maybe she'd earned it. Diana Druid had saved her life, after all. At least once, possibly twice.

"Did you spend the whole night downstairs in the shop?" Helene asked. She sat down and took a deep, welcome drink of her coffee. *Sweet nectar of life, get into my veins,* she purred to herself.

"It's only been four hours," Diana said. She sat down in the other chair and sniffed her own coffee, which was black. "But yes. I did some reading, some visiting with the resident spirits, and I took a nap in that big chair in your back office. Nice little place you've got down there."

"Thanks. Now do you want to talk about what's going on?"

"We never got around to looking into Francine—"

"Fuck Francine. I mean what's going on with you. That book showed up, then you showed up and burned the book, and the book didn't stay burned. That book somehow forced me to read it. Now suddenly Francine can manifest in my apartment, when she's never done that before, and slimy monsters are destroying my carpet. So talk. Tell me what I'm dealing with down there."

Diana looked down at her coffee. Her eyes were neither angry nor ashamed, just terribly sad. She took a sip of her coffee and began.

"I wrote *Imprisonment of Hope* forty years ago, when I was twenty-five. I've been trying to destroy it ever since. I don't know why it manifests the way that it does, or how the King can manipulate people from within. I don't know if it's me, or the book, or the place where it was written. But this is probably the worst possible place it could have ended up, because like you noticed, burning it doesn't seem to work anymore. I think—I hope—that it's because I'm finally down to the last copy, and the King won't go without a fight."

"Where did you write it?"

"Prison. I murdered my uncle."

Helene dropped her coffee cup, and it tumbled onto its side. As she grabbed a kitchen towel and caught the spreading mess before it could spill onto the floor, Diana went on.

"He had it coming. He raped my little sister, and she later committed suicide. That's why the judge only gave me ten years. I served eight. But they were such violent, angry years; I was fighting and spending so much time in solitary…. Finally I put all that rage into the book. When it was accepted and published, I felt vindicated. Like somehow what Barbara and I went through finally meant something. But it only sold a few copies, and the publisher dropped me. I never wrote the sequel."

"I'm sorry to hear about your sister. But why burn the book?" Helene threw the wet towel into the kitchen sink and poured herself another cup of coffee.

Vellichor

"I don't remember very much about the beginning." Diana ran a finger around the rim of her mug. "I was addicted to heroin for a few years after they let me out, and I think I was in a hospital for a while. But I remember the dreams. The Dragon King was coming for me, all my rage and hate made real and coming home. Some of the people I knew, friends who had bought the book, they started getting sick. My friend Marie said the book was too good, and that's why it didn't sell. The Dragon King was too real. Two days later she ended up in the hospital. Sleepwalking. She'd walked in front of a car. I got into her house and found her copy of the book. I burned it in the barbecue pit out back."

"Did she get better after that?"

"I don't remember. I think so. Her husband was mad at me, said I'd broken into their house looking for drugs. Marie wouldn't let him press charges, so I think maybe it did make her better. But I took off after that. I knew what I had to do."

There was a long silence while the two women drank their coffee and contemplated the nature of reality. If Helene hadn't experienced so much weirdness herself over the last year, she would assume that this woman was dangerously unhinged. But she'd been in the presence of the Dragon King. She'd heard his voice. Of course there was always the chance that she was just as insane, and they were sharing a hallucination. Maybe there were no ghosts or books that came to life in her shop. Maybe she and Diana were two crazy peas in a psychotic pod.

Diana contemplated her past and wondered how much to tell her new friend. She hadn't told the full truth: she remembered everything that had happened in the years since she'd been let out of prison. What she didn't know was how much of it was real, and how much was a dream. She remembered burning books, and that was probably real. She also remembered witches and fairy creatures coming out of the handwritten pages into her dark cell to dance with her. And she remembered the Dragon King's handsome bastard son, Reuben Dark. She remembered red hair, and broad shoulders. Was that real, or a dream? Or maybe some fantasy that had helped her through those lonely years in prison. Either way, she didn't think Helene needed to hear any of it.

The women sat and drank their coffee, and the minutes ticked by. Nibbles whistled and rumbled in her cage, rooting around for the last scraps of breakfast before she settled down for a long nap.

Finally Helene asked, "So why are you fixated on Francine?"

"It's hard to explain," Diana said slowly. "But—doesn't she seem angry to you?"

Helene's brow furrowed. Angry? Passive aggressive, maybe. Strangely ungrateful, even after Helene had repelled the boogeyman for the hundredth time. Deeply obnoxious, with her fixation on marriage and makeup and shoes.

"If she died angry, she could be a power source for the Dragon King," Diana explained. "It could explain why the book couldn't be burned. He thrives on rage and death. I'm in a position to know."

"She didn't seem angry talking about it." Helene thought she'd sounded like a ditzy teenager, romanticizing some random booty call she'd run into just before dying.

"There are all different kinds of anger," Diana said. She drank the last of her coffee and got up to put the cup in the sink.

Helene dumped the rest of hers out. She felt sick to her stomach.

She found her laptop computer where she'd left it on the floor, and logged Diana in to a search engine. Funny how things change, she mused. So many adventure movies in the eighties had key moments of discovery taking place in museums and libraries. Now they could probably find out everything they needed to know without ever leaving the apartment.

Helene wasn't that interested in what Diana thought about Francine. She thought the whole thing was a side track. Francine wasn't an angry ghost. She'd never so much as thrown a book in the year that Helene had owned the place. Weren't angry ghosts supposed to be vengeful and destructive, like poltergeists or banshees?

Francine couldn't throw anything. She could stand on the floor and lean on the furniture, but she couldn't lift or manipulate anything physical. So she certainly wasn't a poltergeist. Diana had to be barking up the wrong tree.

She went into the bedroom and scooped Nibbles into her arms. The fat old pig purred as Helene scratched her behind the ears and under her chin. Nibbles had been a birthday present six years before, from an old boyfriend long gone. His name had been Cody. Sweet guy, but he'd liked his weed just a little too much and his job just a little too little. When he'd gotten high and eaten her entire stash of specially imported jelly candies, that was the final straw. But she'd kept Nibbles. She'd feared that Cody would eat her too.

She put the pig back and wandered back into the living room. "Find anything?" she asked Diana.

"Not much," the witch answered. "The party's too old to have left much of an impression on social media. If it had just happened recently you know we'd have video, posts, photos, all sorts of stuff. All I'm finding here are old news tidbits, and they didn't seem to know much. Nothing at all about Francine herself. If we're going to learn about her, we'll have to do it the old-fashioned way."

"Tarot cards and chicken guts?"

"Not that old-fashioned, but you're on the right track." Diana closed the browser and snapped the laptop shut.

"Ouija board?"

"Hell no. We're not that desperate yet." She set the computer down on the coffee table and stood up. "I don't need any tools for this, but I do need you to show me the oldest part of the building. Something that hasn't been rebuilt or remodeled. Preferably not even repainted."

"That's easy." Helene showed Diana to the back of the apartment, behind the door leading downstairs to the shop. "This wall right here is part of the original construction. See, you can see the bricks along the bottom of the floor."

Diana squatted down and touched the bricks. "There are scorch marks right there." She pressed down with the palm of her hand. "It remembers the fire, but I don't know if it's going to be able to give us much detail. There were so many people here that night. Helene, please hold my hand. I'm going to go in a little deep, and I might need you to pull me out."

"What's that mean?"

"Just don't let go." Diana took Helene's hand and squeezed. Helene squeezed back. She hoped Diana knew what she was doing. She had a sense of dark things going on around her, as though she were riding in a canoe over a very deep lake.

Diana sat down cross-legged on the floor, and Helene mimicked her. Diana stared hard at the blackened waves on the chipped bricks, then she closed her eyes. Helene watched her, and while it appeared the older woman was doing nothing but sitting still, that sense of happening was stronger than ever.

It felt as though she was watching events unfold through a thin curtain, or feeling for objects through a felt blanket. Something was happening here, or something had happened and was happening again. Helene's heartrate accelerated. Faintly she heard Nibbles chitter and wheek as she rattled around in her cage.

Helene could almost hear her heart thumping in her ears, and her cheeks felt flushed and hot. It was so hot in here, and the smell of smoke was choking her. Was she afraid? The building was on fire; she should be terrified. But she wasn't afraid. She was angry. So fucking angry. Her rage burned so hot, she felt like it was feeding the flames around her. She remembered who she was; she remembered what she had once been. Now she was nothing, just a forgotten memory with no agency of her own. Something dark and ugly was close by, and it was trying to get closer. Her anger was feeding it. It would make her strong.

"Helene!" Sharply, straight into her ear like a needle.

Helene jumped and released Diana's hand. The witch pulled away and shook her hand gingerly. "I brought you along so you could pull me out if I went too deep, but you almost dragged us both down. Why didn't you tell me you're a natural empath?"

"A what?" Helene blinked and looked around. Everything was normal. It was just her beat-up old apartment, with its leaky roof and cracked drywall. There was no fire, no rage, and no dark presence.

"Because you didn't know. But I should have. Everything in this place points to it. Huh." Diana clambered to her feet. "I want to go finish that bottle of wine. It's five o'clock somewhere."

Chapter Six

They drank in a calm silence broken only by the gentle tinkle of refilling glasses and the warbling chirps of Nibbles. Diana drank the wine; Helene stuck to grape juice. It tasted a bit like wine, close enough to make her feel like she was drinking the real thing.

"I wish Christopher were here," Helene said.

"Tell me about him," Diana said. "Did he take an interest in the phenomena going on in your shop?"

"Not at all." Helene was still tired from the late night, and she felt as though her brain was stuffed with cotton. Ordinarily she was loathe to even mention Christopher to a relative stranger, but she had a bad case of fuck-it this morning. "When I started seeing characters, he thought I needed to go back to the doctor and have my meds adjusted. But I didn't want to do that, because that shit makes me so groggy all the time, like I've been hypnotized and sedated. I'm taking as low a dose as I can get away with now, and that's working out pretty well. I didn't want to do anything to mess with that. Still don't."

"If he thought you were hallucinating, why do you wish he was here?"

"Arguing with Christopher was the best thing in the world when I was confuzzled and muzzled." She was feeling a little punch drunk. She needed a nap. "He made me think things through careful, because he'd shut down any mushy gushy gut reaction. If he were here right now, I'd be telling him what's what, and then I might really know what's what."

Diana nodded. "Sounds like a fun guy to hang out with."

"Oh, he was the worst." Helene flapped a hand. "But he was the best, too. I miss him."

"I'll help you get him back." Diana patted her hand. "I have a feeling that defeating the Dragon King once and for all will hold a key to getting your man back from that black-robed bastard."

"You think so?" Damn. Helene was out of juice. She stared longingly at Diana's wine bottle, but she didn't dare. Another patient of Dr. Clark's had wound up in the ER after an impromptu birthday celebration.

"It can't be a coincidence that he called me here, that the book showed up here. Somehow my problem is related to your problem."

"How do you know?" Helene stuck out her tongue and licked at the bottom of her glass, and Diana gently took it out of her hand.

"Because this has happened before. The book winds up in the hands of a natural witch, and something leads me to her. Or him. I almost always find out that the witch has some sort of psychic problem that I can help them with. Yours is just… a little more than I bargained for, this time."

"Can you help me with my problem, then?"

"Probably." There was an ounce of wine left in Diana's glass, and she polished it off with a hurried gulp. "Now," she said, "I suggest we relax and get as much rest as we can. I'm going to try something a bit risky with Francine, and it's best we do it at midnight for best results."

"What's that?"

"I want to try to exorcise her from the shop, to lay her to rest. Her soul needs peace. It might release some of the rage we felt in the building and reduce the King's power."

"You think she'd be on board with that?" Helene wandered into the living room and plopped down on the couch. Thank goodness the shop was closed today. She couldn't handle other people right now.

"How could she not be? Eternal peace is all anyone wants out of death. Now what do you do around here for fun? We have some waiting to do."

"Well for now I need a nap, but wake me up in two hours so it doesn't screw up my sleep cycle. Later, I'll introduce you to my good friend the video game system. Have you ever played a video game called Fireblast?"

"I don't really play video games."

"Prepare to be schooled."

****

Fireblast was a hit. By the time midnight drew close, Diana's machine gun warriors had picked a dozen of Helene's dragons out of the sky like daisies. After her fourth straight defeat, Helene put down her controller and said, "What time is it?"

"It's twenty 'til," Diana said. She set her own controller on the coffee table and flexed her fingers. "We don't have time for one more round?"

"I want to get something to eat first." Helene went to the kitchen and rummaged around in the fridge as though she didn't have the contents memorized. She could never just pick something out, it seemed. She always had to check, just in case something new had materialized by magic. She remembered her mother asking snidely if she was trying to air-condition the kitchen, and she smiled a little.

It had been two years since her mom had died of cancer. It still felt like yesterday.

Nothing in the fridge but leafy greens and carrots: guinea pig food. But there was a stray can of spaghetti shaped like bug-eyed cartoon characters, and Helene snagged it. "You want to split this?" she asked Diana.

Diana sniffed. "Before a magical ritual, I only consume pure, natural foods. Do you have any kale?"

Helene froze, and Diana laughed. "Kidding! Where do you keep your bowls?"

Once the canned pasta mush had been heated up, served, and consumed, Diana wiped her mouth and said, "All right, time to go. Do you have enough salt and holy water downstairs?"

"I keep tons of it, because of the books," Helene said. She put the bowls and spoons in the sink, where the sauce would harden into red concrete and inspire new heights of profanity the next time she washed dishes.

"That's all we'll really need. Some witches like a lot of flash and dazzle, but I'm more of a get in, get out kind of girl."

"Oh really?" Helene grinned.

Diana held up her left hand. "Really. Look, no tan lines."

Downstairs, Diana looked around the shop.

Vellichor

"Probably the biggest space is the children's area at the back of the shop," Helene said. "There's a big circular storytime rug back there."

"Sounds good. You go get the water and salt and meet me back there. Come running if you hear me scream."

Helene didn't like the sound of that, and she bolted for the office and pulled the two-liter jug of holy water out of her mini-fridge. (It didn't need to be kept cold, but Helene found that anything left lying around her office tended to get buried in books.) Then she found the canister of salt and jogged back to the children's section. Diana sat in the wooden rocking chair and rocked slowly back and forth. Her eyes were closed, and she looked as though she was meditating.

A little brown stuffed bear danced from paw to paw behind Helene's feet. "What's going on, Miss Helene?" it asked in a mild, babyish voice.

"Go on home, sweetie," Helene told the teddy. "And tell everyone to stay in their books tonight. We're doing something a little scary."

"Yes, ma'am." The bear tiptoed away into the shelf behind it, and Helene sighed. Diana seemed nonchalant, but Helene had never seen a true exorcism and had no idea what to expect. Everything in pop culture indicated that even the most routine ritual was fraught with danger.

"Francine… Everywoman… come forth," Diana said. Her voice was sharp and commanding, the voice of a high school gym teacher confronting the class dawdler. It was a voice that tolerated no resistance, and there was none. Francine stepped forward out of nothing to stand before Diana. She tugged at the cuffs of her Victorian costume but said nothing. She didn't seem curious or puzzled by the witch's summons.

"Helene," Diana murmured. "Make a ring of salt around Francine. Between us."

Helene obeyed, but she asked, "Why? Francine isn't dangerous. Is she?"

"Just a precaution. When you open a door into the next world, sometimes things will try to sneak in." Then to the dead woman she asked, "Francine, do you seek peace and freedom from all your earthly woes?"

"I do," Francine said.

"Do you wish me to release you from your pain and your anger?"

"I do."

"And do you accept the power of the light into your soul, driving out all darkness and desire for revenge?"

"I do."

Diana raised her right hand and held it aloft in the vicinity of Francine's forehead. But, Helene noticed, she kept it outside of the salt circle.

"Then Francine Everywoman, I release you. Let go of your anger, and let it dissolve into the shadows. Enter the light, and be at peace."

Francine raised her face to the ceiling and held her arms out as though asking for a hug. A faint, shining light passed over her face, and she smiled. Then the light faded, and she opened her eyes. "No," she said.

Diana blinked. "What?"

"No," Francine repeated. She clenched her hands into fists, lowered them, and flung them open as though she was throwing something. A hot gust of air blasted through the shop, and the salt scattered to meaningless dust.

"My true love won't let me go. He needs me. I can feel him calling me, begging me to stay." Francine's eyes glittered like obsidian, and Diana took a step back.

Helene could scarcely breathe. If salt couldn't contain her, would holy water work any better? Helene was afraid to try and fail; she was terrified of this strange specter who bore no resemblance to the flighty, nervous young woman she'd been. But something would work, something Helene had would repel any creature of evil intent regardless of its power. And of course it was all the way at the front of the shop.

As she dashed away, she hoped like hell that Diana wouldn't think she was abandoning her. Faintly she heard Diana ask a question, and Francine laughed. "You'd like that, wouldn't you?" the dead woman asked.

Helene rummaged desperately in the cabinet beneath her register. She shoved the pistol aside; that would be no good on a dead person. But the silver bearings were a different story.

A month after Christopher's disappearance, Helene had bought herself a sturdy slingshot at a sporting goods store. She grabbed that and the box of bearings. Hopefully Diana had managed to hold it off—whatever it was—long enough for Helene to help.

When she returned to the children's area, Diana was in a wide-legged fighter's stance, her hands waving and gesturing at the air as though fending off a swarm of bees. Francine hadn't moved, but an errant breeze rustled the hem of her dress.

"Francine!" Helene shouted. She set the box of silver down on the floor and took one out. "Who's your one true love? What's his name?"

Francine turned around and grinned at her. Her nose was pouring blood, and her face was blotchy with bruises. One of her teeth was missing. This is what she looked like when she died, Helene thought sickly.

"You'd like that, wouldn't you?" she repeated. "You want his name so you can steal all his power away and send me back to Hell. Well fuck you, Helene. You're not the only one around here who's lost someone special, you ungrateful bitch!"

Helene nocked a bearing in the slingshot and pulled it back as far as she could. "Go in peace, Francine," she said. "Please."

"There is no peace!" Francine screamed. "I've been there, I've seen it! And I'm not going back!"

"I'm sorry," Helene said, and she loosed the silver bearing.

It struck Francine directly in the chest, just above her amply displayed bosom. A small black hole appeared, and Francine stared down blankly. She touched it, and her fingers came away bloody.

"Does your one true love like to read?" Helene asked. "Has he ever been here? Has he ever bought anything, or sold books to me? Please, help us help you!"

Francine only stared. "What happened?" she asked. "Why—why does my heart hurt?"

A shadow fell across her face. Francine looked up—and screamed.

Vellichor

The boogeyman's black shroud stretched across the far wall and most of the ceiling. His long, needle-sharp claws reached for Francine as his withered face grinned and licked his chops with a wormlike tongue.

"Delicious," he hissed, and the dead woman was enveloped in the flowing black shroud.

"No!" Helene screamed. She grabbed more bearings and fired, pulled back and fired, wishing that slingshots came in full auto. Most of her shots went wild, but one flew into the darkness of the boogeyman's cloak, and he roared.

Diana was still chanting and gesturing madly, but it seemed to do no good. "Let her go!" Helene screamed, and she picked up the box and flung the remaining projectiles as hard as she could at the boogeyman, who was now shrinking and dwindling away, flowing like smoke past Helene and back to the front of the store.

"Too late, little witch," the boogeyman taunted. "She's mine now. But don't be sad. Now loverboy won't be lonely anymore."

A tendril of blackness brushed Helene's cheek like a soft finger. She screamed and turned away, and when she looked back, all was still.

The boogeyman was gone, and so was Francine.

Chapter Seven

Helene and Diana stared at each other in empty, shocked silence. Finally Diana said, "So—now what?"

"I don't know." Helene walked around the children's area and picked up as many of the silver bearings as she could find. She didn't need some toddler popping one in his mouth.

"I think we need to go back upstairs and talk a little more. Take stock and figure out our next move."

Helene looked up from the brightly colored ABC rug, where half a dozen silver balls were scattered like marbles. "No. What I need to do right now is go home and go to sleep. Then I am going to wake up, drink a pot of coffee, feed my guinea pig, and come down here to open the shop. I am going to have one halfway normal day before the shitstorm starts up again."

"But the Dragon—"

"Isn't going anywhere. Neither is the boogeyman. Francine is either gone forever or she's not. Either way, she will keep for one more day while I get my head on straight. Just like Christopher."

"All right." Diana suddenly looked very old. And tired. "I guess I'll get out of your hair. I'll go find a hotel to crash at, give you some space."

It was evident that Diana was hoping that Helene would say, No that's not necessary, you can stay with me… but that was not how she felt just then. As a matter of fact, it felt very necessary.

"Come back some time when the shop is open," Helene said. "We can talk then. But right now—I really need a break from all this."

"I understand." She probably didn't. Diana had been waging a nonstop battle for years. She probably wouldn't know a day off if it punched her in the face. But Helene escorted Diana to the front door with as friendly a smile as she could muster, before she checked and double-checked all the locks, reinforced the salt barriers, and headed upstairs for some much-needed shuteye.

Nibbles chirped softly as Helene wandered into the bedroom and crawled into bed. The cool pillow felt so good on her burning face. Then the world around her went black as Helene's consciousness fled.

****

She didn't want to move. She was so warm, so comfortable, and her pillow smelled like lilacs and clean sheets. Vaguely she knew that the real world was waiting for her close by, but she turned her face away and squeezed her eyes shut. Not yet. It wasn't time yet.

"It's all right." Christopher kissed her ear. "You don't have to get up yet."

Helene sighed. Christopher was here, which mean that she was still asleep and dreaming. Good. She snuggled into his warm, welcoming arms. She wished she could sleep forever.

"I know, baby. I miss you too. We'll get through this, and you'll save my ass just like always.

You've always been a fighter, even when you were a kid. Remember that thing with your mother?"

"Not the same," Helene murmured. But she smiled and snuggled in closer. He was still wearing the T-shirt and khaki shorts he'd been wearing when he was taken, which meant they should be getting pretty gamy by now if he was real. But Helene pressed in close and breathed deeply, and she still smelled nothing but lilacs. Not even a wisp of his natural body scent. She swallowed a lump in her throat. So close, and yet so far.

He stroked her hair. "No, it's not the same. But you're a fighter. You went to bat against your own mother, and you'll kick ass again. You're tough."

Helene's mother Brenda had harbored the standard resentments and moody flashes that came with one's husband running off with a call girl in Florida. But then Helene's dad, a well-groomed man with the unlikely name of Huntington, had come back and tried to sue for joint custody of Helene. Brenda had retaliated by threatening to accuse him of molesting their daughter.

Up until that point Helene had always tried to accommodate her mother's strange and sometimes irrational ideas, but when she'd overheard Brenda talking to her cousin about it, she'd hit the roof. She'd told her mother off, clearly and concisely, and finished with the announcement that she would tell Huntington everything if she didn't knock the crap off and stop standing in the way of her father's attempts to reconnect. After two weeks of cold silences and clipped words, Brenda had calmed down, but it had taken Helene years to forgive her.

Dr. Clark had helped; having a safe outlet for her frustrations had helped her put a lot of anger to bed.

"You went to war against your own mother, and I know that wasn't easy," Christopher said softly. "You kicked ass then, and you'll kick ass again. And now you've got help. I'm glad Diana showed up when she did."

"She said you called her." Helene put her hands around his waist. He felt so real in her arms. She never wanted to wake up.

"The boogeyman keeps me inside his Book, but I can sometimes see what's going on in the real world. Like light through a curtain. I knew you were in trouble, but I couldn't get to you while you were awake. But I could see Diana clearly. She was like a beacon reaching way up into the stars. She was looking for that book, and I showed her where it was."

"How?"

"I don't know. It was all in my mind, like how you act when you're dreaming."

"The boogeyman ate Francine. He reached right through a circle of salt. How did he do that?"

"I don't know," Christopher repeated. "But I think she's distracting him. I've been lying here with you for a long time, and he hasn't pulled me back yet."

"I wish you could stay." Helene squeezed his hip, then ran her hands over his firm ass.

"Me too. But it's time to wake up. You've barely eaten in two days, and it's time to open the shop." Christopher leaned down and gave her a long, slow kiss that made her toes curl. "I'll be back soon, baby."

Helene's eyes flew open, and she groaned with frustration. Nibbles' bright black eyes peeked at her through the cage bars, and the guinea pig wheeked hopefully.

Her arms were sprawled, empty, on the bed. Christopher was gone. He'd never been here. Just a dream, like all the others. Helene had only her own relentless hope that the dreams were real enough to mean that Christopher was still alive.

Nine in the morning. The shop opened at ten today, which gave her an hour to eat, shower, and open the register. At least she didn't have a commute to worry about.

She dragged her ass out of bed and, blurry-eyed from heavy sleep, she started a pot of coffee. She hadn't washed the pot the day before, but fuck it. A quick rinse got most of the brown crap out of it, and how germy could coffee get anyway? It wasn't like meat or dairy; it wouldn't infect her if she left it sitting out.

She took history's shortest shower while the coffee brewed. Not to save time or energy, but because the water was unbearably cool. She'd have to get the water heater looked at again. One of the downsides to owning her own property was having to take responsibility for all maintenance crises.

But the payoff was having a business under the same roof, so almost everything she did to the place was a total write-off. She needed a working hot water heater to run a successful business, didn't she? Sure she did. Employees were required to wash their hands. It was in the manual somewhere.

She put on a long black skirt and blouse and ran a brush through her wavy blonde hair. It was no good trying to style it or keep it neat, she'd learned; even the most supernatural-free day would entail climbing ladders, digging through boxes, and all but rolling like a dog in old book-dust. She'd figured out long ago that her best friend in the hair care department was the scrunchie.

She drank her coffee standing up and watching the clock. She didn't want to set foot downstairs until she absolutely had to. At nine-forty she set her empty cup down with a sigh. Time to face the music.

Just before she left, she gave Nibbles an extra carrot and a scritch under her chin. "Be a good baby," she said, and Nibbles purred.

There was a cold draft in the hallway leading down to the shop. It felt as though she'd stepped into a walk-in freezer. "Get out of here," Helene said, her breath puffing from her mouth in a steamy cloud. "If you don't stay out of my personal space, I swear to God I'll burn the whole place to the ground and fly to Aruba on the insurance money."

The chill vanished, and Helene nodded. Of course she would do no such thing, but characters and ghosts shared one common trait: they tended to be one-dimensional thinkers.

It was troubling that they were apparently starting to invade her apartment. They hadn't done that before Diana's appearance. Was her presence giving them strength or courage? It didn't matter, but they needed to stop.

Once she was down in the shop, Helene stopped for a moment just to breathe and look around. She felt like she never did that anymore, never noticed the aromatic scent of old books or the scuffling sound of her feet on the cheap carpeting.

The walls were painted with climbing ivy that surrounded famous literary faces and scenes. There was a portrait of William Shakespeare; over near the children's section was a classic image of Winnie the Pooh. Helene remembered being enchanted by the place as a teenager, and the feeling had returned when she'd come back to move in. But the enchantment had been overcome first by the tedium of running a small not-particularly-profitable business, then by dismay and horror when she'd realized exactly what was living here.

It wasn't all horrible, though, she thought as she returned a wave from an anthropomorphic kitten in a white pinafore. The characters from the children's section were all shy but friendly, and they were a calming presence when she just couldn't take any more grown-up horrors.

Helene wandered up to the front desk and turned on the computer, which powered the register. She went through the comforting routine of firing up the register and counting the cash inside. It felt good to do something so mind-bogglingly boring. Having to constantly change tracks and plan for the worst was exhausting.

"Hey, Helene," said a young woman in a paisley shawl. She stood a ways off, near the shelf labeled New Arrivals. Her black hair was tied into a pair of tight braids that looked like they hurt her scalp.

"Oh, hi." Helene smiled. It was one of the hippie hitchhikers. "Jazz? It's Jazz, right?"

"Right!" Jazz sidled closer. "I like your place. It's a nice break from—"She tossed her chin back, toward the shelf behind her.

"From all the drama of your own story." Helene had heard that a lot. Once or twice she'd been asked if Enchanted Ink was heaven.

She wondered what happened to the characters' consciousness when the book was bought and taken out of the shop. They seemed like real people here and now, but as far as she knew it didn't last once the book was taken away. Nobody had ever called the shop complaining about the ghosts that had come with the merchandise.

Did the characters have souls? They seemed capable of independent thought, though that depended on the quality of their creator. Did they have any real agency, or was it all an illusion? She'd never heard a character express dismay or fear about being bought. And she'd never have a book come back after being purchased, so she had nobody to ask what it was like. She wondered if it felt like dying.

"Hey Jazz," she said casually, "what do you remember from before you came to the shop?"

"I'm sorry?" The hippie was touching one of the walls, tracing the ivy around and around a painting of The Bard.

"You manifested here two days ago, along with your friend with the blonde hair. Do you remember anything from before you showed up? Did you exist, before?"

Jazz closed her eyes and took a deep breath. She pursed her lips and blew as if trying to whistle. Or blowing out pot smoke.

She said, "I think I existed, but I don't remember what it was like. I feel like I was swimming, like a fish. I wish I could smoke a bowl. Pot always helps loosen my synapses."

"Huh. So maybe you reincarnated from another form? Maybe you really were a fish."

"I don't know. Like I said, I don't remember. I think I was happy. I don't know why I'm here now."

This was the most information Helene had ever gotten from a character, so she didn't push it. She went back to work.

Jazz watched as Helene went about her morning routine: setting out the day's clearance cart, picking up stray books that had fallen off the shelves (she felt that this happened an inordinate amount of time, despite the fact that the spirits here seemed to have no power over physical objects) and turning the sign from CLOSED to OPEN.

Finally Helene took a deep breath and unlocked the door. *Let the wild rumpus start,* she thought.

Nothing happened, of course. Customers would trickle in and out throughout the day; hers was not the sort of business that had long lines of people beating the door down at opening time. But still, Helene felt a sense of free-fall when she opened that door. Now that the outside world had been invited in, anything could happen.

"Hello there," Jazz said to someone behind her. "Welcome to Enchanted Ink."

Helene turned and opened her mouth, ready to remind the hippie that most customers couldn't see her. But of course it wasn't a customer; the door hadn't chimed. Helene's eyes met those of a shaggy-haired young man in a faded concert T-shirt and blue jeans. His face was clean for once: no bloody nose.

"Oh hi," Helene said. "I haven't seen you in a while. Sorry, I forgot your name?"

"Harold." The dead man took a deep breath and looked around. "I never noticed how good it smelled in here. It smells like a library."

"Usually when I see you there's blood coming out of your nose," Helene commented. "It probably feels good to have clear sinuses for once."

"Yeah, it does." Harold breathed deeply and smiled at Jazz. "Hi there." A note of shyness. "Are you new?"

"Yeah." Jazz nodded at the New Arrivals shelf. "Where are you from? Your hair is weird. Like, sort of grey. But not old people grey."

"I'm not from a book," Harold said. "I died here. About thirty years ago? There was a fire. I hit my face, and there was blood everywhere."

"So you died in the same fire that killed Francine." Helene's skin prickled. "Can you tell me anything about it?"

"No, sorry. I was really, really drunk. I fell down in the ruckus and passed out. Never felt a thing. I just remember blood pouring out of my nose, and then fade to black."

"Well if you've gotta die that's probably the way to do it," Jazz said, patting his arm.

"Yeah, I guess. And before that kooky witch asks, I'll pass on the exorcism. I saw what happened to Francine last night."

Helene lowered her eyes. They'd only meant well for Francine, but she had to admit they'd tried to lay her to rest for nothing but selfish reasons. She felt ashamed.

"Oh hey, I'm sorry," Harold said hastily. "I know you didn't mean for that to happen. But man, that boogeyman. You gotta get him out of here."

"I know. I just wish I knew how to get Christopher out of there first. And Francine."

"You think she's still—you know, real?"

Helene thought about it and nodded. "I don't think he'd take her just to destroy her. That would be too easy on me."

"Yeah, he likes to fuck with you, doesn't he? He did the same thing to your Aunt Sarah."

Helene nodded again. "That's why she had such an arsenal stashed around the shop. But I don't know why she didn't burn the book. I would, except for Christopher."

Harold shrugged, but Jazz said, "Maybe she did. Like how the witch tried to burn that."

They all looked at *Imprisonment of Hope*, still lying on the counter where Diana Druid had dropped it. And set it on fire. But here it was. Some books, apparently, could not be burned.

Chapter Eight

A few customers came and went over the course of the morning, and Helene basked in the normalcy of their presence. Two were casual browsers who had never been to the shop before; they exclaimed over the wide selection of classics and the crawling ivy painted on the walls. "Who did the decorating in here?" asked the purple-haired young woman. Her partner, a young man with a green Mohawk, snapped a picture of a row of first editions.

"I don't know," Helene answered. "It was like this when I started working here."

"This place is badass," the young man said. "I feel like I could just hang out here all day and read. Soak up the vibe."

"I feel the same way," Helene said with a smile, and she wished them well as they departed with promises to return after payday.

"You should have told them that the painter mysteriously died two days after completing the last wall," Jazz said from behind her left shoulder.

Helene snorted. "Why?"

"It would give them a thrill. They were dying for you to tell them a ghost story, couldn't you tell?"

She hadn't, but she always felt out of touch these days when she interacted with normal people. Sometimes she felt like she was a ghost herself, watching the real world pass by outside the bright windows.

So a book character was better at reading people than a live woman. That was little unsettling.

The third customer came and went right before lunch time: an elderly who came every two weeks like clockwork and combed through the children's section. Usually she took picture books and board books—always quick sellers because of how expensive they were when brand new—but today she added a stack of young adult fantasy novels.

"My daughter just got a new foster child, and she's a little older," she explained as Helene rang her up.

"I hope she enjoys the books," Helene said. "That'll be twenty-two, ninety-eight."

The lady handed her twenty-five dollars in cash. "Do you know if any of these characters have black characters? The foster child is black, and I want her to feel—represented."

"Um." Helene had never been asked that before. "I haven't read any of these, so I couldn't tell you." She picked up one that had NOW A MAJOR MOTION PICTURE stamped in gold foil on the cover. "I saw the trailer for this movie though, and one of the actors is—African American." Helene stumbled over the words, feeling impossibly white.

"I guess that will do." The old lady gathered up her purchases and put them into the cloth bag she carried everywhere. "Have a good day now." She nodded to Jazz. "You too." And she left.

Helene stared at Jazz, who stared after the woman as though she had sprouted wings. "She saw you," Helene said.

"Groovy," Jazz breathed.

Vellichor

Normally customers brushed right past the ghosties and ghoulies that manifested in Enchanted Ink, though occasionally one would pause and shiver if they made contact. That old woman might have some sort of second sight, or witchy power like Diana. Helene wondered how she'd react to some of the vintage science fiction characters who sometimes played cribbage or poker in the little-used romance section next to her office.

But now it was lunch time, and Helene was hungry. She hadn't eaten on a proper schedule in several days, and her stomach seemed anxious to get back on track. She headed back to the office in search of sustenance.

The bell over the door jangled as she headed back up front with two granola bars, an apple, and a bottle of plain old unholy water. Diana Druid stood just inside the shop with her hands in her pockets and an apologetic expression on her face.

Vacation's over, Helene thought sickly, and she set the food down. Suddenly she wasn't hungry anymore.

"Hello," Diana said.

"Hi." Oh fuck it. Helene sat down on the stool next to the register and opened her first granola bar. Life wouldn't get any easier if she passed out from low blood sugar.

"I found a nice motel over in Hillsdale," Diana said. "About ten minutes away. Nice little place. Clean."

"That's a rare and beautiful thing," Helene said as she bit down. Chocolate chip. Her appetite came roaring back, and she gobbled it down in three bites.

She paused to take a breath after swallowing the last chewy bite. "So what now?" she asked. "I'm a little afraid to ask, considering how well your last idea went down."

Diana flushed, and she dropped her eyes. "I deserved that."

Then Helene felt bad. "No, you didn't know." She tore into her second granola bar. "I think I'm just hungry."

Diana shook her head without raising her eyes. "I should have known. I've never been in a place like Enchanted Ink. I shouldn't have expected anything here to follow the rules I'm used to."

"Do you think Francine is still...?" Helene didn't know how to phrase the question.

"Herself?" Diana opened her hands helplessly. "Ordinarily, I'd say yes. But this isn't an ordinary situation."

"You've never seen book characters come to life before?"

"Not like this. Don't be so surprised. How often do you think this happens?"

"I don't have any idea." The second granola bar was gone, and Helene cracked open her water bottle. "I haven't been able to talk to anyone about this. Just Christopher."

"You never talked about it with Sarah? You said before that you used to hang out here when you were a kid."

Helene shook her head and took a deep, satisfying slug of water. When her mouth was clear she said, "I remember talking about it with her when I was really young, but I also remember that we both treated it like... like it was just a game. A story we told to each other. Then when I got older I got really sick. I was around nineteen when they diagnosed me with schizophrenia. I stopped coming here after that. Mom said I needed to get out more and be around real people so I'd learn the difference."

"Real people?"

Helene flapped her hand. She didn't want to talk about her mother, or those troubled years in which she'd forced herself to adapt and fit in with what Mom called the real world. "I do have a few ideas, though."

"How have I not asked this before? Fire away."

"Idea number one." Helene took a bite of her apple. "This happens everywhere, in all book stores, and nobody ever talks about it."

"How existential. I love it. Go on."

"Idea number two. This shop is some kind of gateway between dimensions, and energy is bleeding through and taking the shape of the images in the book."

"Formless energy from another dimension that can read. I love it even more."

Helene raised an eyebrow. "Are you making fun of me?"

"No, no." Diana shook her head vehemently. "It's just my gallows humor. When I'm scared and don't know what to do, I crack stupid jokes."

"Fine." She took another bite of apple. "Anyway, my last theory is about something called ley lines. Are you familiar with them?"

"A little, yes."

"Do you know if they're real?"

Diana hesitated, then said, "I don't know. I've read about them, but mostly in fictional stories. And those fluffy, flowers-and-fairies Wicca books mention them. But most books about magic get at least half of it wrong, so who knows?"

Now that Helene was talking about this out loud, ideas were popping together like bubbles. Or maybe it was finally getting some decent food into her stomach.

"What if," she said around a mouthful of apple, "ley lines were places where that raw energy is bleeding through? Like our own world is shifting tectonic plates, and the lines are cracks between? And that shit's bleeding through in this spot, in my shop."

"Interesting thought." Diana took a stick of gum out of her pocket and opened it slowly. After popping it into her mouth and chewing for a minute or two, she said, "I don't know if any of this helps us, though. Your defensive magics seem to maintain the peace, but I don't have the slightest idea how to banish the evil. I don't know any of the rules of this place, and I'm not sure we have time to learn."

"You don't know the rules," Helene said softly. She glanced over at the front desk, where *Imprisonment of Hope* still lay. Neither of them had touched it since Diana's attempt to burn it. As Helene watched, the cover rippled slightly, and Helene smelled brimstone.

"What are you thinking?" Diana asked.

Helene went over and touched the book's cover. It felt warm, as though it had been sitting in the sun. She pressed down on the cover as though feeling for a pulse, and something hard and bumpy slid away under her fingers.

She looked up at Diana. "We don't have time to learn the rules. The boogeyman has Christopher and Francine, and the Dragon King is only one sentence away from escaping. I can feel him under there, the real him, not a character manifestation. It's like a dog with a worn out chain about to break."

"I know all that. Get to the point." Diana's tone was harsh, but her face was alight with hope.

"We don't have time to learn the rules. Well— what if there are no rules? What if we don't know the rules because we need to make our own?"

"How?"

"You have to write the sequel. You have to write a sequel to *Imprisonment of Hope*."

Diana stared at Helene. "Are you fucking nuts? The last time I wrote a book, it woke up and started hurting people. If I write a sequel, that would just give the Dragon King more power."

"I don't think so. I think it would bring him back under control. *Imprisonment of Hope* ended on a downer. The dragon won. People were dying. They were running up against those walls that were supposed to protect them and crushing each other trying to get out. It was hell on earth—or wherever the Walled Kingdom is."

"I know how the damn thing ends. I wrote it."

"So write another one that ends differently. Bring hope back to the Walled Kingdom. Bring back that baby who's supposed to grow up to kill him. Fix the mess you made."

"I can't control the ending of the book. I can't promise to make things better."

"No, but you certainly can't make things any worse."

Diana sighed and looked Helene in the eye. "Have you ever written anything?"

Helene hesitated, then said, "Yes. I used to write all the time, when I was a kid. It helped me deal with some of the weird stuff going on. Aunt Sarah encouraged me. She thought it was helping."

"What made you stop?"

Helene's heart thumped harder. She didn't like to talk about it. "I got scared of the stories I was writing. One of them was really bad, and I wrote it while I was sick and having trouble—dealing with reality. It gave me—nightmares. That was the last story I ever wrote, right before my diagnosis. And it was the only story I ever published. Go figure."

"So you know how it feels to write a story, to have this entire world under your control… only it's not under your control. You're just holding on for dear life and writing everything down as it comes. You know how scary that can be."

"Of course. But Diana—what choice do we have? The alternative is basically to hang out and wait until that dragon finds a new way out of the book. Isn't that pretty damn scary too?"

Diana stared at her. Then, slowly, she nodded.

****

Helene's computer in her office was equipped with three different word processors, but neither of them trusted the machine to do what they needed. "These characters manifest from paper and ink books," Diana said. "I don't think one has ever appeared out of an e-reader or smart phone, has it? Electronics don't have the right kind of magic."

Helene's own reasoning was far simpler. She wanted Diana to write this next book under circumstances identical to those when she'd written *Imprisonment of Hope*. That meant an outdated electric typewriter and cheap paper. If she could have had Diana sent back to prison as well, she might have considered it.

No, not prison. Prison was full of anger and hate, which was exactly what they were trying to dispel. Diana needed to be surrounded by love and hope, which meant that she needed to be surrounded by books.

She toyed with the idea of providing Diana with her old manual typewriter, an Underwood from the fifties she'd bought off the Internet because it looked exactly like one that her favorite science fiction writer used. But that was probably too old-school. It would drive Diana crazy.

There was a thrift store four doors down from Enchanted Ink, called One Man's Treasure. Helene flipped the OPEN sign to CLOSED, added a small white placard that said BACK IN FIFTEEN MINUTES! and headed down to rummage through their electronics. Diana stayed behind to settle into the office and familiarize herself with the ergonomic chair.

"Hello there!" chirped an older woman with glasses so large and thick that her eyes seemed to dance in her face. "I haven't seen you for a couple of days!"

"I've been a bit distracted," Helene said, the understatement of the year. Instead of heading for the milk crate full of moldy hardcovers and trade paperbacks like she normally did, Helene wandered to the back of the store, where they kept old electronics. She'd found a couple of outdated but still playable game consoles there before, with games that had been a pleasant day trip down memory lane.

And wonder of wonders, among the broken monitors, digital cameras, and sepia-colored printers (the kind that printed on spooled paper with those long strips full of holes that were so much fun to tear off), there was an electric typewriter. She hunkered down and picked it up.

"Are you finally going to write one of your own?" the older woman asked from Helene's left shoulder.

"Oh no," Helene laughed. "This is for a friend of mine."

The older woman laughed with her. It was a running joke between them; the shop assistant (whose name Helene had never learned and was now too embarrassed to ask) insisted that anyone who spent so much time around books should be able to write one of her own. Helene had retorted that that was like expecting a car salesman to be able to drive like Dale Earnhart. She'd be damned if she was going tell a relative stranger about her early attempts at writing. Nobody ever looked at her the same way after they found out.

Helene lugged the bulky old thing up to the register, just then remembering to ask, "Do you know if this thing has ribbon? Or ink, or whatever these things used to run on?"

"Ink ribbon. And you're in luck. The lady who donated it also donated a few boxes of ribbon. Apparently it was in her attic forever; her son wanted to be a novelist. But he never finished anything, and it just took up space until she finally cleaned up there and here it is."

Big Eyes took a plastic bag full of small white boxes from behind the register and laid it down next to the typewriter. "Altogether it's five dollars," she said primly.

Helene handed her a ten from her wallet. As Big Eyes rang it up and counted her change, Helene thought of something. "Dr. Dixon's office isn't still open, is it?"

"What? No, it's been closed for five years, at least. Way before you took over the shop. How do you even know him?"

"My aunt went to him. When I was a kid and used to visit her here, we'd walk past his office and she'd say, 'There's my doctor. He's a peach. If you ever get a good doctor who makes you feel like a person and a patient, you hold on to him like a good boyfriend.'"

"That sounds like something she'd say. But no, Dr. Dixon passed away, and his office closed. He'd had just delivered his nine hundredth baby."

"I'm sorry?" Helene blinked.

"Dr. Dixon was an OB/GYN."

Chapter Nine

"So the guy who gave you that box of books was lying," Diana said thoughtfully.

The two women were like archeologists at an ancient site, poring over the electric typewriter like an artifact from a different world. Which in a way, Helene supposed it was. She remembered life before the Internet, but it was like memories from early childhood: foggy and not quite real. Her father had always owned a computer as far back as she could remember, but it had held no interest for her until she was about ten and had a random question about bats. Mom's response had been, "Let's look it up on the Internet."

And thus, Helene thought with amusement, an addiction was born.

"He was lying for sure, but what a weird lie," she said to Diana. "He didn't even need to tell me he was going to the doctor. Why make up a story that I could find out was fake? Did he just lie for kicks?"

"I don't know. It's weird, though, you're right about that. Should we try to track this guy down?" As Diana spoke she fiddled with the buttons and switches on the back of the machine, most of which served no visible purpose. She was older and remembered using machines like this, but even she had to fumble around with it before she finally remembered how to install the ink ribbon. Then she sat down in Helene's comfortable leather chair: a rare extravagance that Christopher had insisted on.

Vellichor

("Be nice to yourself for once in your damn life, Jesus!" had been his exact words.) Then she rolled a sheet of crisp white paper in, centered the page, and typed, Chapter One.

"Now what?" Diana asked.

Helene was dumbfounded. "What do you mean, now what? Now you write the book."

"I don't know what to write."

"I'm sorry?"

Diana turned to her. Her face was naked with fear. "I haven't done this in thirty years. I've had a million ideas since, but I never wrote them down. I don't think I know how."

Helene was nonplussed. She had no idea how to respond. Her own writing back in the day had been easy, just free-form stream of consciousness fiction full of princesses and unicorns and talking dogs. (Until it had turned darker and grown teeth, but she refused to think about it.) She hadn't realized that it was possible to lose the knack, and it unnerved her. How could Diana not know what to write? If Helene ever picked up a pen again (perish the thought), would she find that the words had deserted her as well?

She said the cleverest thing that came to mind. "What?"

Diana turned back to the blank page. "It's so white. And empty. I don't remember the page being so big before."

"It's always been eight and a half by eleven, hasn't it?"

Diana put her hands over her face, and her shoulders trembled. Helene wasn't sure if she was laughing or crying. Maybe both.

Dawn Napier

That was the first awkward silence of their entire relationship. Diana sat in the leather office chair, covering her face as though hiding from the blank page. Helene stood behind her in helpless silence, racking her brain for words of encouragement. Or an opening line. Something. Anything she could say, she felt, would help. But her tongue felt locked, her mind as blank as the page in the typewriter. She no more knew what to say than Diana knew what to write.

"Hello, Earthlings." Helene turned and smiled at the handsome young man in the silver space suit. He set his fishbowl down on a nearby table and ran his gloved fingers through his neatly trimmed black hair.

"Hi, Roger." Helene was genuinely glad to see him. He hadn't manifested since his near-miss with the boogeyman last week.

"Roger?" Diana turned around and studied the silver-clad hunk. "Where are you from?"

"Vintage science fiction." Roger grinned and cocked his thumb behind him. "First edition."

Diana chuckled. "No, I mean what planet. You look human."

"I am, but my parents were the first generation to colonize the fertile belt of Venus. All of my adventures take place between Venus and Mercury."

"Did you ever make it back to Earth?"

Roger frowned. "No? Yes. I don't remember, but I think I did. Or I will. It's confusing."

"It's probably in a book that I don't have in stock," Helene said.

"Maybe. Mostly what I remember is flying around in the military warship, zapping big blue bugs out of the sky."

Diana's eyes crawled over Roger's silver-clad body. "Do you have a lady friend?"

"Diana!" Helene put a hand to her chest, feeling like a dowdy old lady but unable to help herself. "He's not real!"

"Oh hush." Diana flapped her hand. "That's not what this is about. Do you, Roger?"

"Marla." Roger smiled vacantly. "Beautiful girl. The daughter of my CO. Smart, too. Fastest typist in the solar system."

"Anything bad ever happen to her?"

"Well, she keeps getting kidnapped by her father's political enemies…"

Helene wandered away. The doorbell chimed, and a young woman with three lively little boys burst in. Helene said hello, and the mother gave a very distracted wave as she trotted nervously after her scampering menagerie. The boys seemed to know where they were going; they made a beeline for the back of the shop. Maybe they could see what Helene saw: three waving teddy bears and a sparkling spider-web that stretched overhead reading SALUTATIONS. The children could sometimes see them.

The boys never seemed to stop moving, but Helene was pleased to see that they appeared to respect the books. The oldest was around seven or eight, and he showed his brothers picture book after picture book, putting them back carefully when the younger boys were through. "No, not there, it goes there," he corrected the youngest, sliding a book with a red dragon on the cover into the correct slot. "Hayden, don't bend the book like that, you'll break it!" he scolded the middle boy.

"He's your little helper, huh?" Helene said to the mother, who was trying to browse the nearby literary fiction while still keeping them in sight.

"He's been Mr. Independent ever since he learned to walk," the woman said. "Do you have any Barbara Kingsolver?"

"Right over here," Helene said, and the woman promptly emptied the shelves of every copy. "Wow, big fan, huh?"

"She's the best. Boys! Pick one book a piece and follow me."

"You got more than one book," the middle child objected, and the older boy glared at him.

"I pay the mortgage," Mom responded. "If you don't like my rules, you can put your book back and go home with nothing!"

"Sorry," the boy muttered, and he picked up a bright yellow picture book with a black dog on the cover.

When Helene was done ringing up their purchases and saying goodbye to the loud but lovable children, she headed back to the office to check on Diana. Roger was gone, but Diana was hunched over the typewriter, and—Helene's heart thudded with relief—it was clacking. There was one full sheet of paper on the desk next to her, and the sheet inside the machine was rising steadily.

Helene didn't want to disturb her, but she didn't want to leave either. She found a stool under the table and sat on the edge of it, feeling out of place in her own office. There she sat as the afternoon wore on, and Diana filled three more pages, front and back.

Roger manifested several times, just watching Diana type along with Helene. He glanced down at her, and Helene looked back up at him. He opened his mouth to speak, then shook his head and retreated. Weird.

Helene got a few more customers before closing, mostly window-shoppers. She was zeroing out the register and the credit card machine when the clacking suddenly stopped. Helene had gotten so used to the constant noise that she jumped a little when it ceased. Then Diana came out of the office looking like she needed a cigarette. "That," she said slowly, "was amazing."

"Did you get a start on the book?" Helene asked. Finally, she thought, finally there was a beginning of the end of this craziness.

But Diana said, "No. Haven't started yet. I just finished a little story about Roger and Marla. It's very sweet. Eventually. He had to kill a lot of blue bugs first."

"Um." Helene took a breath, let it out slowly. "Um. Why? What was the point of writing about Roger? I thought you were writing a sequel to *Imprisonment of Hope*." She was trying not to sound angry and failing miserably.

"To break the block. The book is too big. I couldn't just jump into it without any preparation. Not after being away from the typewriter for forty years."

"I see. So it's a good story?"

"I have no idea. But I finished it. I finished a story. Would you like to read it? I need an outside opinion."

"Of course." Helene locked the front door and changed the sign. Then she went back to the office, where her leather chair was still warm.

The story was five pages long, double-spaced, front and back. Helene sat and read the whole thing straight through, hoping like hell that the story was at least decent.

And it was. More than decent, in fact. There were spelling and grammatical errors, and there was one page where Diana had briefly fallen in love with the word "suddenly." But the story itself was both action-packed and charming. It started out predictably enough, with Marla being stolen away by an evil scientist who was manipulating the blue bugs for some nefarious purpose. Roger was able to win the day and rescue the fair maiden, and in an amusing twist she was able to rescue him back when one of the bugs tried to infiltrate his warship and catch him off-guard. Diana's description of the scantily-clad warrior maiden blasting the bug's head off its thorax made Helene smile and feel warm. She could feel Roger's affection for Marla flooding through the page.

When it was over, Helene looked up to see Roger standing next to her. "Do you know what she wrote here?" she asked the star man.

"I lived it," he murmured. "I lived it while you read it. I could feel it becoming real. I haven't felt this real in over fifty years. I feel—possible."

His face glowed with religious ecstasy. "Would she write another one? Ask her to write another one. Please?"

Oh, dear. "She has something else to write, something really important," Helene said gently. "But I'll tell her what you said."

"Would you read it again? Slowly this time. I want to feel every word. Marla is so beautiful."

"It would be my pleasure."

And it was.

Chapter Ten

At the front of the store, Diana lingered near the register, dancing from foot to foot like a teenage boy asking a girl out. "What did you think?" she asked.

"I liked it." Helene grinned. "I think it might be better than the original book."

Diana visibly relaxed. "So I still have it," she said. "I can still do this. Can't I?"

"I don't think it's anything you can lose. It's like riding a bicycle." She hoped.

Diana shook her head. "I don't know about that. But I'm glad I can still do something. And now I'm hungry. I don't feel like I'm going to vomit anymore, and my stomach is screaming at me."

"I'll order something for delivery." Helene pulled her phone out of her pocket. "There isn't much to eat upstairs."

Dinner was shrimp-fried rice and egg rolls from the little storefront Chinese place four blocks away. The owner, Chuck, waived the delivery fee since it was such a short run, and Helene promised him a discount on his next purchase at the shop. Chuck said he'd swing by when it came time to do his Christmas shopping, and Helene laughed.

Diana didn't start the book that day, but Helene still felt encouraged. The writer's spirits were up, and she circulated the shop happily, browsing through the books and chatting with characters. Roger hovered close to her like a star-struck fan, which made Helene smile. The shop had an atmosphere of celebration, which the customers seemed to feel as they came and went. Almost everyone found what they were looking for or something close to it, and the two or three who didn't still left smiling and promising to return.

While Diana was living it up among the stacks, Helene turned on her personal computer and browsed the Internet. She realized that she hadn't checked her email in almost a week, which meant that her inbox was almost certainly full. Being a small business owner meant getting a lot of spam and other crap, but it also meant that she had to sort it very carefully lest she miss a marketing or sponsorship opportunity that could bring in some much-needed revenue.

Ten offers of "anonymous hookup with horny housewife." Those she could safely drop into the SPAM folder, where it would disappear forever. Coupons for heating and air services she held onto, just in case. A local library was putting on some sort of event for underprivileged children and wanted to know if she could donate some books. Helene sent back a brief message requesting more information.

More horny people, both men and women, a request for her banking information so she could receive a hefty settlement from a lawsuit she didn't even know existed, and about a dozen special offers for goods and services she'd never heard of and would never use. Helene was about to Select All and dump the whole mess when she saw a message from Uncle Brach. Holy shit.

Technically he wasn't her uncle; he and Aunt Sarah had been married for three turbulent years when Helene had been a teenager. But they'd stayed in touch over the years, exchanging letters and later emails a few times a year. But Helene hadn't heard from him since she'd inherited the shop, and in light of recent events she'd sort of forgotten about him. She felt a bit ashamed. It was one thing to lack the time to write, but she hadn't even thought about him. She'd seen him at Aunt Sarah's funeral, but he'd stayed only for the ceremony and left quickly as soon as it was over. She remembered seeing him standing at the back of the church, looking sad and out of place in a navy blazer with black pants. When the procession had begun, Helene had stood up to look for him, but by then he was gone.

"Uncle Brach," she said aloud. "How the hell are you?"

Well, it was time to find out. She opened the email.

Hello, Helene,

Hope all is well with you. And the shop is holding up okay. I lived in that apartment with Sarah while we were married, and it is very nice and cozy. It was right after she bought the shop. We had big dreams of running the shop together and then selling it to you and retiring to Florida when we got old. Turns out neither of us was cut out for marriage, but I do miss that book store. I love the smell of old books.

I am still in touch with your cousin Tess, and she sends her love. She married some sort of animal doctor and lives in Arizona now. It's so funny how we can be scattered all over the country but still talk to each other instantly with email. Now Tess says nobody emails anymore, and she's going to teach me how to text. But fuck that. I found something that works for me and I'm not changing again just because I can.

Tess's father passed away. Pancreatic cancer. That one's a bitch, kills just about every time. He had a lot of bad habits that probably didn't help, either. I don't know if you knew him all that well, he and Sarah were together just long enough to make Tess happen. I did see him at the funeral though. I don't know if he was sick then or not. I didn't find out until after it was over.

Anyway, say hello to everyone in the shop for me. I always liked reading to those little limey boys. And Roger—is he still there? He's a sweet fellow. I hope you're keeping that asshole boogeyman under control. He always gave Sarah hell, especially around Halloween.

All my love,
"Uncle" Brach

Helene read the email three times. She wasn't sure if she was surprised or not. She thought she might be beyond surprised. She just felt sort of—glowy.

The little limey boys.

Roger.

That asshole boogeyman.

Brach had known all about the shop. And he'd never said a word to warn her.

But really, what could he have said? Would she have believed him? Of course not. She would have assumed that he'd fallen off the wagon again, or that he was humoring her delusions. And everything would have happened just the way it had happened.

She hit Reply.

Hello Uncle Brach. So sorry we haven't been in touch. Tell Tess I'm sorry about her dad. The boogeyman is being the biggest asshole you can imagine. Do you have time to talk? I have the same cell as last time you called.

Thanks, Helene.

She headed back to the office to check on Diana. She was hunched over the typewriter again, and the keys were chattering away. Helene gently tiptoed away.

By the time she got back to her computer, Brach had replied.

Fuck that. Meet me for coffee. Sacred Grounds about ten minutes from the shop. Meet me there about eight. You're already closed, right?

She smiled as she responded.

I'll be there. I may bring a friend, if she's not working.

Then she shut the computer off and sat on the stool behind the register. So Brach was back in town. How long had he been around? And why had he not gotten in touch sooner?

Well, she'd find out at eight o'clock, apparently.

****

Vellichor

About an hour later, the soothing clack of the typewriter trailed into silence, and Diana reappeared. Her face was bright, and her eyes shone. "Are we closed?" she asked.

"Yep. Start the book yet?" Helene asked.

Diana shook her head. "I've just been writing a few random scenes, bits and pieces of different things. I'm flexing my muscles, getting back in shape. But I think I know how to start it." She stretched, and something popped. "Ugh, my back."

Helene's phone beeped, and she said, "Why don't you help me wrap up the store, and we'll go for a walk. Stretch our legs."

"My everything needs stretching." Diana grinned. "That sounded dirty, didn't it?"

Helene snorted. They don't make old ladies like they used to, she thought.

She'd already zeroed out the register, so she finished shutting down the computers while Diana drew the blinds. It felt weird to lock the doors and then go out the front door; she normally just went upstairs for dinner. Nibbles was going to be pissed.

The evening was cool and comfortable, the sun inching towards the horizon in an orange blaze. "Looks like October," Diana commented, admiring the orange cast to the sky.

"Yes, it does. The trees will be turning soon. I love Halloween, but I hate the cold so I never know how to feel about fall."

"You do anything for Halloween in your shop? Put all the horror novels on sale, anything like that?"

"Yeah, I have sales for just about every holiday. And the kids come trick or treating around town, so I put out goodies."

103

"Real goodies or pencils and book marks?"

Helene rolled her eyes. "Real goodies. I like my windows egg-free."

Sacred Grounds was a coffee shop-dash-bakery that Helene had taken Christopher to on one of their first dates. It was a little painful now to open the door and step into the wave of warmth and the scent of coffee. Helene breathed deeply; she also smelled sweet cinnamon. The owner, Sharon, must be turning out a batch of fresh cinnamon rolls.

"This place is magical," Diana murmured.

"I know," Helene answered. "Wait until you taste their mocha."

"No, I mean it's really magical. Like your shop. There's a presence here."

Helene swallowed. Just once, she thought, let me relax and enjoy a damn cup of coffee without something supernatural jumping out at me. "What kind of presence?"

"Nothing malignant," Diana said quickly. "It's comfortable. Positive energy. Just big."

"Well there's nothing wrong with something big and friendly living close by. My neighbors had a Saint Bernard when I was a kid. Her name was Cupcake." Helene stepped up to the register and addressed the owner's purple-haired daughter, Rachel. "I'll have a twenty-ounce café mocha, and one of those cinnamon rolls I smell."

"And I'll have the same." Diana reached for her wallet. "Let me get this. It's the least I can do after everything."

"Thanks." Helene looked around. There was no sign of Brach, but it was just now eight o'clock. He usually showed up twenty minutes late to everything.

"Is everything all right?" Rachel asked as she rang up their purchases. "I haven't seen you in here for a while."

"Everything is fine," Helene said with a smile that felt as real as a supermodel's cheekbones. "It's just been a busy couple of days, and Aunt Diana here came for a visit. Showed up unannounced. Threw me for a loop."

Rachel didn't seem to know how to respond to that, so she finished printing the receipt and wandered away. Helene and Diana exchanged an awkward glance, and Helene shrugged.

They found a table, and just as their food and drinks arrived, so did Uncle Brach. He manifested in the doorway like a raggedy wizard from a fairy tale. He was older and thinner than Helene remembered, but unmistakably the same crazy old man Aunt Sarah had married. Which husband was he? Third? Or fourth? Helene couldn't remember; she didn't think she'd met them all. And maybe the ones she had met hadn't all been legal husbands. Or her legal husbands, anyway. Helene's brain was starting to hurt. Her mother hadn't approved of Aunt Sarah's lifestyle, so they had only attended her first wedding.

But Brach was the only one with whom Helene had ever felt a kinship with, and the only one she had willingly called "uncle." And he was the only one who had bothered to keep in touch after fleeing Sarah's marital bed.

"Uncle Brach!" Helene said, rushing in for a hug. The older man hugged her back fiercely and kissed the top of her head. He smelled like weed and incense. God, she missed Aunt Sarah.

Diana, meanwhile, looked up from her cinnamon roll with a smile—then did a doubletake. "Well, this is a nice surprise," she said. Her face was completely blank. "Helene, you didn't tell me we were meeting an old friend this evening."

"I'm sorry. I didn't' think it was a big deal. Brach, this is Diana. She's a writer, and her book is haunting my shop. Diana, this is my uncle… who you apparently already know. Um." Brach and Diana were staring at each other like cats meeting for the first time. If Diana had a tail, it would be lashing.

Brach extended a hand. "Nice to see you again, Di."

"Likewise." Diana's face was pleasantly neutral.

"I'm just going to go get a coffee," Brach said. Under the white bristles adorning his face, he was deeply scarlet. "I'll be right back."

Helene and Diana sat down to their coffee and rolls. The cinnamon smelled just as heavenly as ever, but Helene's appetite had taken a back seat to her curiosity. "So how do you know Uncle Brach?" she asked. She tore a small strip off the edge of her roll and delicately picked out a raisin.

"How do you?" Diana took a sip of coffee and kept her eyes down.

"I've known him since I was a kid. He used to be married to Aunt Sarah. Now dish."

"We dated off and on for a few years. Probably before his marriage to Sarah. And a bit after."

Helene frowned. "And during?"

Diana would not meet her eyes. "Maybe. I'm not sure."

Helene gritted her teeth. "Did Aunt Sarah know?"

Diana shrugged and bit into her cinnamon roll. She looked like she was trying to hide behind it.

Well, the only person who could be hurt by this was dead, so Helene told her angry nerves to chill out. Water under the bridge. She ate the strip of roll in her hand and tore off another. Brach joined them with an enormous coffee confection topped with whipped cream and chocolate shavings, and they ate and drank in a silence that was only mildly uncomfortable.

When her roll was nothing but a sweet memory and a tiny pile of raisins on her plate, Helene took a draught of her cooling coffee and addressed her uncle. "So what brings you back to town? Do you know what's been going on in the shop?"

Brach's straw rattled as he sucked a glob of whipped cream through it. "Only that the auras in this town are getting agitated. That usually means that the boogeyman is acting up again."

"So you know about the boogeyman. You know about the book characters in Aunt Sarah's shop."

"I started seeing them right after Sarah and I got engaged. Is Roger still there?"

"Yeah. He's got dozens of books, and every time I sell one, I get two more the same week. I don't think he'll ever leave. Diana wrote a story about him."

Brach stared at the writer. "Did you write it in the shop?"

Diana's brow furrowed at his expression. "Yes. Why?"

"He's probably there to stay now, even if all of his books get sold. Writing—it does something in that place. Makes things real."

"That's what we're counting on." Diana filled him in on Helene's ideas and what they planned to do to finally neutralize the Dragon King.

Brach scooped another glob of cream into his mouth using the end of his straw. "This could work. This could actually work. How can I help?"

Helene blinked. "I—I don't know."

"That's why I came, Leenie. I knew you were in trouble, so I came to help. Tell me what to do."

Diana leaned forward. "Tell us everything you know about Enchanted Ink. Every manifestation you've ever seen, everything Sarah has ever told you. And I can't believe you never said anything about this to me before! You knew I was hunting for that damn book!"

"You always told me shut up whenever I mentioned Sarah's name."

"You should have tried harder." But Diana's eyes flicked away. Helene shook her head. The Other Woman expressing righteous indignation. That was rich.

Chapter Eleven

Brach Whalen had been seeing things that weren't "real" all his life. When he was old enough to visit the library by himself, he did his own research on hallucinations and the mental illnesses that could cause them. He'd decided on his own that he didn't need professional help. He had no delusions of grandeur, no paranoia, and he was fully capable of functioning at work and school. The prismatic colors and winged creatures that he saw occasionally never affected him in any way. So he mostly ignored it and went on living his life. At fifteen he'd made the mistake of confiding in his girlfriend, and she'd told her parents that her new boyfriend was schizophrenic. Word had gotten back to his parents as well as all over the school, and it had taken days to convince everyone that he'd only been joking with her. She'd offered him a blowjob as an apology, but he'd been too mad to enjoy it.

But lesson learned: trust no one with weird secrets. It was a lesson he took to heart and lived by for years, until his volunteer work brought him to Life Beyond Bars: a program that provided books and care packages for women in prison. He became pen pals with a confessed murderess named Diane, and after her parole he took a leap of faith and decided to meet her.

"You told me they were stories you made up in your head to keep you from going crazy with boredom," he said wryly to Diana. "But the stuff you pretended to see looked an awful lot like the stuff I saw every day."

They had never had a formal relationship, but Brach and Diana had been on-again, off-again lovers ever since. Brach didn't think he'd ever meet someone he could love half so well until he met Sarah Glover. He met her while scouring local libraries and book stores in search of cheap reading material for the inmates, and they too had struck up a friendship that became something more.

"When did you realize that the book store was haunted?" Helene asked.

"The day after I proposed to her. I was there past closing time, and one of the monsters pulled a stunt. I want to say it was a werewolf. It jumped out at me and pretended to bite my throat."

Brach had been browsing through the science fiction and horror. The prison wouldn't allow anything too "emotionally disturbing," but Brach was hoping to find something for himself for once. He'd touched an old paperback with a wolf on the spine, amused by the gaping jaws and dripping blood. The things people found scary in the seventies.

"It felt gross," he said. "Like I was touching something dead. And then this thing jumped out from between the shelves. It was huge, and it had the oversized jaws just like the wolf on the spine of the book I'd just touched."

Helene shivered. Some of the books on that shelf had the same feel; she didn't like touching many of them. She thought that might be why horror novels usually didn't sell well; even non-sensitive customers could feel it.

Vellichor

"I don't remember what all happened after that," Brach continued. "There was blackness everywhere, like someone turned out the light. Then when they came back on, I was sitting in a chair in Sarah's office, and she was holding my hand. She asked if I was all right, and I said sure, I just got a little dizzy for a second there. And she said, 'Those fucking monsters. Most of them just want to be left alone, but some of the stories just demand to cause trouble.'"

Brach slurped some more of his coffee milkshake. "Not much more to tell. We were in love, and we were married a while, but it didn't work out. Maybe we were too different. Or we had all the wrong things in common."

Helene asked, "When did you first see the boogeyman? You mentioned him in the email."

Brach studied her for a long, careful moment. "It would have been right after Sarah and I split. You were spending a lot of time in the shop, I remember. I thought it was to comfort Sarah, but she said you were dealing with your own stuff at the same time."

"I was. I got bullied a lot all through school, and it—it got bad there for a while. I had—lots of bad feelings. But I never had them at Enchanted Ink. I could hide from the bullies there, and it felt like I could hide from my feelings too. It was my safe zone."

"Did you ever see the boogeyman while you were there?"

Helene thought about it. "No. I didn't start seeing characters until I took over the shop. And even then it took a while for them to show themselves. I don't think the boogeyman was even there when I was a kid. The copyright date on that book is from the year I started college."

Helene drank the last of her mocha. "So what brings you back now? I could have used your help after the funeral. Christopher—" She shook her head.

"I'm sorry." Brach rubbed his eyes. "I was drunk. I was heartsick. I thought I'd only get in the way. I should have come back as soon as I knew you'd inherited the shop. But I didn't know you were sensitive to it. I thought you'd be okay."

"Sensitive to it?"

"Only certain types of people can see the characters, and only people who can see them can be affected by them. I always thought that was why Sarah didn't leave the place to her own daughter. Tess is highly sensitive. The place would have eaten her."

"Christopher wasn't sensitive. He always thought I was making up stories because I was bored all the time."

Brach shrugged. He picked up his drink and upended the last icy dregs into his mouth. "I never knew Christopher personally. I don't think we ever met. Maybe he was and didn't admit it. I only know what Sarah told me, which wasn't half of what she knew, I'm afraid."

Helene was silent for several minutes, absorbing what she'd been told. Brach and Diana exchanged a few complicated glances, engaging in a conversation that flew over Helene's head. She didn't care. Their weird relationship drama was at the very bottom of her list of concerns.

112

Finally she asked her uncle, "So why are you here now? What good do you think you can do now, when it's too late to stop Christopher from being taken?"

"I don't know. I just got a feeling. They're usually right."

Helene stared at him, and then she shrugged. "Well, it's good to see you again, anyway. I'm going to head home and feed Nibbles. We'll talk some more tomorrow after I open."

"It's good to see you too," Brach said. He smiled shyly at Diana. "And you. It's been a long time."

"Time really gets away from you, doesn't it?" she said. "It feels like just a few months ago."

Their eyes continued their silent conversation, and Helene felt herself blushing.

"Where are you staying?" Diana asked Brach. "Maybe we should talk some more."

"Yeah, I really need to get going," Helene said quickly. See you lovebirds tomorrow."

****

Helene didn't dream about Christopher that night. She dreamed about Francine.

"Tell that witch to get her ass in gear," she said in Helene's ear.

Helene sat up in bed. She was in complete darkness, though she had left the hall light on as she always did. Either the light had burned out, or she was still asleep.

"Tell her," Francine repeated. There was an edge in her voice that gave Helene the cold shivers. Francine had never spoken to her like that before. She'd never sounded strong.

"I know she needs to start," Helene said to the darkness. "She's just rusty. She hasn't done this in a while."

"Then dump some oil on the bitch!" Something struck Helene across the face, and she cried out. "Sorry, sorry." The darkness swirled around her like black mist. "But you're running out of time. The boogeyman has me. He's feeding on me. He plans to use me to challenge the Dragon King, and I don't know what will happen if he wins."

"If he kills the Dragon King, that's half my problem solved," Helene said. There was another stinging slap and a tug on her hair. "Ow!"

Francine's voice was low and close to her ear. "The Dragon King is the embodiment of hatred and rage. The boogeyman feeds on negative emotions. You know what he's capable of. You know better than anyone. Are you sure you want this to happen? In *your* shop?"

Helene imagined a machine gun with unlimited ammunition. Or a nuclear device powered by the sun. She shook her head silently.

"Then tell that witch to get to work."

Helene's eyes darted open. On top of her dresser, Nibbles' black eye appeared, and the pig chirped hopefully. Helene hadn't even moved yet. How did she always know?

Helene sighed and sat up. Dreams like that always left her feeling ill-rested, as though she'd lain awake all night with her eyes open. But she usually had the comfort of Christopher's touch and smell to make her feel better. Not this time. All she had was guilt, fear, and a warm spot on her cheek where Francine had slapped her. Bitch.

Vellichor

Not that she didn't have good reason. Francine had been an angry spirit, carefully concealed under a passive-aggressive exterior, and she had plenty of reason to be even more pissed off. And if the dream was true, she was currently serving as the boogeyman's all-you-can-eat buffet. God only knew how long she could survive in such a state. Could the boogeyman just... eat her soul? Consume her completely until there was nothing left? If so, that would be on Helene's conscience.

Helene dragged her ass out of bed and dumped a fistful of pellets into Nibbles' cage. The pig cocked a bright eye at her, possibly wondering why Helene wasn't chirping back or babbling baby talk. Helene scratched her behind the ears. "Don't mind me," she told the furry little lump. "I'm having a week."

Fresh coffee brightened her outlook on life considerably. Over her second cup, Helene decided that Francine was right. Diana needed to get to work on that sequel. No more bits and scenes, no more fan fiction about Roger Starr. It was shit or get off the pot time. Helene was going to put her foot down if Diana tried to put it off again.

Helene drank her coffee, stared at the hideous green kitchen wall (that was beginning to crack, goddammit), and thought about Francine. Before Diana's appearance, she'd never given the dead woman a lot of thought. Francine had always seemed to go out of her way to be obnoxious and superior... the perfect cover, Helene realized. If Francine had been friendlier, Helene might have tried to get to know her and learn about her past. And Francine had clearly had no interest in letting anyone into her life.

She told herself that that this meant that learning everything about Francine would likely provide a key to stopping all of this bullshit and getting Christopher back. That might be true, but as she rinsed her coffee cup she forced herself to face an ugly truth: she wanted to snoop because Francine didn't want her to.

Well, hell. It wasn't as though she had much else to do. Diana was about to start writing the sequel to *Imprisonment of Hope*, and once she did Helene didn't know what she could do to help besides keep the protections up and stay out of the way. Why not engage in a little detective work as well?

She grabbed a piece of bread from the cabinet over the sink and smeared it with peanut butter. She shoved it into her mouth as she locked the door behind her and trotted downstairs to the shop. By the time she reached her register the bread was gone. She hadn't realized how hungry she was. Helene wiped her fingers on the front of her blouse and commenced the start of her day.

By the time she flipped the CLOSED sign to OPEN, Helene knew where she ought to start. The strange man who had donated the box of books. He'd dropped them off without waiting for her to even look at the books, let alone open an account for him so he could get store credit. And he'd lied about where he was going afterwards. That didn't mean he was somehow connected to the supernatural goings-on, but it seemed like a good place to start. Weird coincidences seemed to be the order of the day. What were the odds that her favorite uncle had spent the best years of his life banging Helene's favorite author behind Aunt Sarah's back?

Speaking of the perverts, neither of them had showed up yet. Helene glanced at her back office, where the electric typewriter waited. Francine had been right. This needed to start today. Helene couldn't have said exactly what was so special about today, but her gut insisted that it was the day.

A few window-shoppers wandered in and out without buying anything, and about an hour into the day Roger manifested at her right shoulder. Helene blinked. He looked the same—silver jumpsuit, goldfish bowl under one arm, rugged military good looks—but he was so much more *there*. There were stray hairs sticking out around his ears, and Helene could see the pores in his skin. She fancied that she could almost reach out and touch him.

"Is Diana coming today?" he asked.

"She should be." Where was the old witch, anyway? Probably sleeping off a sex coma.

Roger took a deep breath and let it out. He looked like a man breathing fresh mountain air rather than a stuffy old book shop. Helene's heart felt warm and cushy at the sight of him. The whole place might go up in flames at any moment, but Diana had made poor old Roger feel good, and that was a nice thing. Helene thought she'd better appreciate nice things while she could. There might be a shortage soon.

"I can't remember the last time I felt this good," he said. "No offense, but it's been so dull here. Like the colors drained out of my life. But now I actually feel alive. Like I'm more than a ghost of an outdated story that nobody reads anymore. I haven't felt like this since before the fire."

Helene paused, realizing what he'd just said. "You were here before the fire? But Aunt Sarah bought the building after."

"My books were here before then. They belonged to one of the renters upstairs. Nobody could see me—not like they can now—but I still remember."

"How did your books survive the fire?"

"They were in a storage box in someone's closet. The fire didn't actually spread very far beyond a bedroom and the adjacent kitchen. Most of the damage was smoke and water. And of course the deaths—"

"Drunks panicking and trampling each other." Helene lowered her head, thinking of Francine. What a terrible way to die. It made Helene feel bad for thinking such bitchy thoughts all this time.

A trio of little old ladies wandered in, twittering among themselves about the coffee they'd just had. Apparently tasted exactly the same as what they'd had at a café back in Pittsburgh, where they'd gone on vacation. *Who vacations in Pittsburgh?* Helene wondered. *Maybe they'd been visiting family.*

"Young miss, where is your romance?" one lady called over.

"On the far right wall," Helene said, pointing. "Anything in particular you're looking for?"

"Oh no," another chirped. "Marlene just wants a look at your collection of naked man chests." They all giggled.

Helene's face warmed, and she turned away to hide her reaction. They really didn't make little old ladies like they used to.

Once they were safely out of sight, Helene said to Roger, "So you remember the fire. You were there. Kind of."

"Kind of," he agreed. "I didn't see very much. Mostly what I remember is the party. Lots of drinking, people pairing off in every dark corner. It's amazing how many dark corners there are in an apartment."

"Was Francine one of them?"

Roger's eyes went distant as he concentrated. "Yes. She was with the fellow in the creepy dog mask. They were both drunk, I think. And they were doing some kind of sex ritual."

"Ugh." Helene rubbed her arms and fought the urge to cross her legs. "Was she raped? Is that why she was so angry when she died?"

"No, the sex was consensual. But the guy—his name was Reuben—he was in charge of the ritual. But something went wrong. They were calling a dark spirit with their sex energy, and I think something actually tried to come through. They tried to stop it. Or Francine tried to stop it, and Reuben knocked her down or pushed her away or something. A candle got knocked over. I think that's how the fire started."

Why hadn't Helene thought to question the characters before? This was information they probably could have used.

Because it hadn't occurred to her that any of them could predate the book store. She thought the book magic had arrived with Aunt Sarah. Maybe some of it had, but something else had been waiting here for her. Something evil.

Chapter Twelve

Helene's prodigal uncle arrived just before lunch time with a Styrofoam clam shell in his hands. Diana was right behind him, holding another clam shell. Helene smiled at them both and tried her best to ignore the cat-that-ate-the-canary look in Diana's eyes.

She was about to ask them (in as polite a tone as she could muster) where in the hell they'd been all morning, but Brach cut her off with a cheery, "We brought you lunch!"

A whiff of bacon quelled Helene's annoyance. Lunch turned out to be an order of Sacred Grounds' special breakfast potatoes, scrambled eggs with bacon, onions, and cheese. The other clam shell held an enormous cinnamon roll.

While Helene ate (like a starving wolf; she had forgotten how good their breakfast potatoes were) Diana circulated the store and Brach filled her in on what they'd been up to all night and most of the morning.

"We've been talking to priests," he said, and Helene almost choked on a potato. "The guy who owns Sacred Grounds used to be in the priesthood. Until he got married and had a kid—or was it the other way round?"

Brach chuckled, and Helene rolled her eyes. She knew this already; the name of the coffee shop was an ironic joke. But she'd never considered turning to the Cawleys for help with her supernatural troubles. It hadn't occurred to her that they would believe her.

"Anyway, Jason dropped in right after you left, and we talked a while. We didn't tell him any of your private business, but we asked him about things like other worlds, other dimensions, demons and ghosts and so on. Just to feel him out, at first. He said he didn't believe nor disbelieve. One of the reasons he left the church—aside from the obvious—was everyone kept expecting him to know everything. And he said he'd seen some things that made him realize that he didn't know as much as he thought."

Helene scraped the last cheesy fragments out of the bottom of the clam shell. "So...?"

"So nothing. We just talked. But he did give us his email address and said stay in touch if we need anything blessed."

"Can he still do that? He's not a practicing priest anymore."

"Catholic doctrine says yes. Once you join, no take-backs."

Helene nodded. She dropped the empty clam shell into the garbage can under the register and started on the cinnamon roll. "I wonder if his holy water would work better than mine. I just bless it myself using a purification ritual I found in one of Aunt Sarah's books."

"One way to find out." Brach pulled a bottled water out of his coat pocket and handed it to her. "I had him to bless this for me before we left."

Helene shook her head and took the bottle from him. "Weirdo," she smiled.

"Hey, Helene?" Diana called from the office doorway. "I'm going to get to work now."

Helene had a mouthful of gooey cinnamon roll in her mouth, so her response was, "Mmph mmph?" But Diana understood.

"The sequel. I got an idea last night. I got an idea, after—we went to bed. I know how to start it now."

Diana turned and disappeared into the office. Helene and Brach stood together in silence, listening. Then it began: the sound Helene had been quietly longing for. The clacking of typewriter keys.

Helene slowly at the rest of her roll and listened to that marvelous sound. It was different from before. Harder, more urgent, as though Diana was slamming down the words and saying, Take that. And that. The sound felt real and sincere and honest. Diana was finally doing what she'd been hiding from for forty years.

Fuck you, Dragon King, Helene thought triumphantly. And fuck you too, boogeyman. We'll kick your asses yet.

****

Customers filtered in and out over the course of the afternoon. Rain threatened but did not fall. Brach settled down in the rocking chair at the back of the children's area and opened an HG Wells novel. And Diana continued to write.

Half an hour before closing time, Roger appeared near the front door. "Someone's coming," he said.

Helene's brow furrowed. People had been coming to the shop all day. "So?"

"I don't know." Roger tossed his fishbowl in the air and caught it. His face was oddly pale. "But suddenly I wish my laser blaster worked in this world."

That gave Helene an uneasy feeling. Even worse—Harold, the bloody-nosed teenager was lurking behind Roger, just to the right of the shelf labeled Local Authors. He only appeared when something ugly was about to happen. He didn't say a word, only looked from Helene to Roger and back again as though silently asking for help.

Her uneasiness turned into actual apprehension when she recognized the ginger-haired older man who stalked through the door. The stranger with the box of books, who had lied about having a doctor's appointment. He had lied for no reason at all, and that bugged Helene more than any sadistic, purposeful lie. She didn't like when things made no sense. It was probably why she was a fan of genre fiction, where everything fit together perfectly.

"Can I help you?" she asked.

"Francine. Where is she?" the older man rubbed and twisted his hands together.

"I don't know—" she started. Then, "Wait, how do you know Francine?"

"She's gone, isn't she? You had her exorcised. I can't believe this." Rub, rub, rub went his hands.

His constant motion reminded her of a homeless woman she'd met at the bus stop when she was in high school. An older woman, like this fellow here, with thin hair and dry, scaly skin. She'd rubbed her hands together too, and scratched incessantly at her arms and ribs. The woman had talked incessantly, continuously, a nonstop ramble about looking for booze and a place to sleep that required no response or even acknowledgment from Helene. She'd only said goodbye when Helene boarded the bus, and Helene had watched her wander away from the bus stop, still scratching and possibly still talking.

It was the same mixture of fear and sympathy that moved her now. The old man was acting exactly like an addict in withdrawal. Now both his hands were in his pockets, as though he was trying to hide them. "We didn't do it on purpose," she said. "I'm so sorry."

"Well I'm doing this on purpose," he said, and he threw a fistful of something black and stinging into her eyes. Helene cried out and put her hands to her face. It was gritty, like dust or sand. Her eyes burned.

"Helene!" Roger shouted, and she felt his strong hand gripping her arm. She didn't think he'd ever touched her before. She hadn't thought he could.

"Fucking bitch," she heard the stranger say.

"Hang on," Roger whispered. "You're going to be all right."

She blinked rapidly several times. Of course she would be all right. It was just some nasty black sand, or maybe dust. Random guy being a prick over something that hadn't been her fault or her idea.

The shop seemed brighter behind the blurring. Almost as bright as the sun outside. As her vision cleared, Helene looked around. Roger was no longer at her side.

It took a moment for her to react. What she saw was so bizarre and unexpected, it took a moment to feel anything.

But was that true? As unexpected as her new situation was, a small voice in the back of her head marveled at the cliché. As soon as Diana had started writing the sequel, she should have been waiting for this.

The sky overhead was clear, brilliant blue, and the sun was a glowing dandelion. It hung in picturesque perfection above a range of purple mountains with snow-capped peaks.

Helene stood on a ledge overlooking a minor gorge. She looked down to see brilliant green foliage surrounding a sparkling stream. The water looked diamond-clear even from this distance, and Helene knew that if she climbed down there and knelt by the stream to drink, she would see tiny glowing fish dart away. They would be all different colors, and if she scooped one up it would dissolve into liquid color and drip back into the water to magically re-form.

She knew this gorge, and she knew those mountains, though she had never seen either one with her physical eyes.

As if on cue, behind her Helene heard the tiny cry of an infant. She turned around slowly. Roger knelt over a battered, woven basket stuffed with grey and black rags. "The princess is hungry," he said.

Helene still felt no surprise. And why should she? This was the world where she'd spent her childhood, comfortable as an old shoe. Roger's silver jump suit was gone, replaced by battered but gleaming armor. His fish bowl was now a helm that lay among the weeds beside him. Helene looked down at herself and saw exactly what she would have expected: a loose, woven tunic of some rough brown material, baggy trousers, and sturdy black boots. Traveling clothes that would disguise her sex from a distance, exactly what she would have envisioned for herself.

The basket of rags squalled again.

"My lady?" Roger said. His face wore none of its usual familiarity; he addressed her as a servant would address his master.

Helene shook her head. "Of course," she said. "We came prepared." Had they? There was a satchel lying on the ground at her side, and when she looked inside she found a leather flask that sloshed when she shook it. She opened it up and sniffed, then she grimaced. Warm milk. She hoped it hadn't soured. She handed it to Roger.

The young man gathered the bundle of rags into his arms. A tiny hand waved from the bundle, and he smiled. "She's looking for it already."

Helene sighed, but she had to smile too. "She's always full of hope. Like her name." Which was Ember, she remembered. She couldn't remember if she'd read it in the first book or not.

Roger helped the baby sit up and suck a little milk from the flask. "Have you seen any of the King's patrols?" he asked without looking up.

"No. So far we seem to be safe. How far until we meet this witch of yours?"

"Herb wife. Hers is the magic of hearth and home. True witches work in fire and—"

"And I don't care." Helene turned away. "I apologize. I shouldn't snap. I'm just hungry. I wish I could live on warm milk and soft bread."

"We should reach Meg's hut by sunset tomorrow. She'll have milk and bread a plenty, and meat for those of us with teeth."

"And a healing poultice for that leg of yours, I hope."

Roger tucked the baby back into the basket without looking at her. "It's getting better."

Helene knew he was lying, and she saw the evidence for herself, when he picked up the basket and they started walking again. The dragon's claw had barely grazed his thigh, but he walked with a limp that became more pronounced with every day. He refused to let Helene look at it, only saying that he was washing it daily and it was healing slowly. Helene feared for him. Not only what would happen to her and the child if he were to sicken and die, but what would happen to his heart and soul if he failed them. If he died thinking himself a weakling, he could doom himself to the underworld. Only true warriors went to the Golden Haven.

But she said nothing. Seeing everything and saying nothing was what had kept her alive before, and she had faith that it would continue to do so. Anyway, why fight about it? Either he would live or he wouldn't. There was nothing she could do either way, and his soul would not be saved by arguing.

They followed the gorge roughly southward, and that night they took shelter in an abandoned hunting shack in the middle of a wood. It smelled dusty and dry, like old books, but it was relatively clean and would protect them from the elements. A cool wind was rising from the west as the sun went down, and Helene smelled rain on the breeze. Dusty or not, they would want the shelter.

Vellichor

Helene took the basket to a far corner and hunkered down beneath the filthy window. She doubted anyone could see inside through the crust of dirt and grease, but she kept herself and the baby out of its line of sight nevertheless. Roger lay across the shack's single entrance, still wearing his rough, dented armor.

The baby slept soundly in the basket, thumb firmly planted in her plump little mouth. She always slept like that, snuggled up among the rags that Roger had gathered from the wreckage of her home. One tattered shirt had been taken from her wet nurse's body, which was likely why the child slept so well. The shirt was dark brown and showed no stains.

The dim light in the shack darkened further, as though a cloud had passed across the moon. Helene blinked and shook her head. "What just happened?"

Roger sat up. "The chapter just ended."

"Excuse me?" Helene looked down at her rough clothes. She pulled at a strand of hair; it was its typical sandy blonde, with her trademark split ends. She was still herself. But where the hell was she?

Roger picked up his helm and studied it thoughtfully. "Clever of Diana to do this. Goodness knows what would have become of us if the dragon dust had succeeded."

Helene leaned over and touched the baby's chubby arm. It felt real enough, warm and alive and huggable as any living baby. But when she snapped her fingers next to her ear, the child didn't even twitch. Dead to the world.

"The chapter's over," Roger said. "It's basically intermission for us. We can talk and move around, but we can't advance the story."

"You're acting like you've done this before," Helene said.

"This is my life, Helene. Where do you think I go when I'm not keeping you company or acting as live bait for the boogeyman?"

"I've never really thought about it."

"You don't think about much besides yourself, do you? Francine, me…"

Helene was hurt. "You could try cutting me a little slack here. I've been through a lot in the last six months. And unlike you, I'm not used to being a figment of someone else's imagination. How do we get back to my shop?"

"I don't know. You know what's going on here, right? You know that baby."

Helene looked down at the child and nodded slowly. "Ember. The baby who survived at the end of *Imprisonment of Hope*. We're in Diana's sequel."

"She wrote us in as guardians of the child. It must have been to save you from the dragon dust."

"What's dragon dust? And who was that man?"

"I didn't recognize him until it was too late. Most of the people I know don't age, and it's been over thirty years since I saw him last."

"That was—Francine's true love? The guy she hooked up with at the party?"

"Apparently when he ran away from the fire he didn't go far."

Helene put her hands over her face and tried to collect her scattered thoughts. Her voice muffled, she said, "So this guy performed a sex rite that started the fire, and then he came back and blasted me with something that sent me into a book. What's his deal?"

"Oh, he wasn't trying to send you into a book. What he threw at you was supposed to blind you and poison you slowly. He was trying to kill you."

"What? Why?"

"He stormed in raging about Francine. Apparently he was as attached to her as she was to him, because he tried to kill you using a highly volatile, very rare substance. It was the magical equivalent of setting you on fire with gasoline."

Back to Francine again. It seemed like everything revolved around Francine lately. Helene wished again that she'd taken the time to get to know the stuck up bitch when she'd had the chance.

"So Diana saved my life by putting me in her book. How?"

Roger shrugged. "I have no idea. She's the witch, not me."

Fair enough. "So now what happens?" She lay down on the filthy floor next to the motionless child. The floor was cool and strangely comfortable.

"Now we do what the story tells us. And hope that Diana's boyfriend puts her in the mood to write us a happy ending."

Helene closed her eyes. It had been a very long day. She thought that a happy ending would come second to just letting all this shit come to an end.

****

Morning dawned, as crisp and golden as an apple. Baby Ember drank a little more milk, and the adults breakfasted on edible weeds that they found growing around the shack. It wasn't at all an appetizing meal; Helene thought longingly of roast mutton and hot bread as she gnawed miserably on her stalks of green. But those days were gone. She was no farmer's daughter now but just another vagabond on the run. She and Roger filled their bellies as well as they could. They would need all the energy they could muster for the last leg of their journey.

They had no fresh diapering material for Ember, so Helene did what they'd been doing for days: she moved the rags around in the basket until the cleanest material was touching the baby's tender skin. The foulest she buried under the leaves behind the shack. It was not a perfect system, and the baby desperately needed a bath, but Roger had said that this witch—or whatever she was—was less than a day away. She would surely have water, soap, and perhaps even cleansing powder for the poor thing's irritated skin.

They took turns relieving themselves behind the shack, and once again they started on their way. Roger was bigger and stronger than Helene, but he was also burdened by his heavy armor. So Helene carried the basket and child, counting the steps in her head and wondering over and over again how such a small person could add so much weight. The basket thumped against her legs on every third step, and she mumbled a string of curses directed at prophecies, wizards, and the world in general.

"It can always be worse," Roger said, catching some of her profanity.

Helene eagerly joined him in their favorite game. "The baby could be crying relentlessly," she agreed. "A high-pitched, shrieking cry that attracts predators."

"Or she could weigh twice as much."

"A crying giant baby… wolf. What if the prophecy spoke of a chosen wolf, rather than a chosen child? How would we feed it?"

"Will a wolf drink milk? We can't even find meat for ourselves."

"But even wolf cubs can walk. I wouldn't have to carry this basket."

"Because it would be chasing you. Trying to eat your ankles off."

"But still—it could be worse."

And on. They left the wood behind and climbed over a gentle hill, and before long they were in a lovely little valley that to Helene seemed specially made for a quaint village. Roger kept one hand on his sword and scanned the sky continuously. By midday his fears manifested.

"Wyverns?" Helene asked as the tiny black dots appeared against the brilliant blue sky.

"Wyverns don't flock. And the Dragon King will keep his highest minions close to him until the threat's been defeated. Those will be something smaller."

"Easier to fight?" she asked hopefully.

"Probably not." And her hopes were dashed.

Roger looked around. "Let's try hiding behind that hill over there. There are rocks everywhere that might serve as cover."

"I wish you could take off your armor," Helene complained as they scrambled over the rocks and settled in among them as well as they could. Roger drew his sword and lay it across his lap. "You'd be harder to see if you weren't so shiny."

"You know I can't. Not until my curse has been lifted," he said.

She sighed. That cursed curse. Who knew that attracting the ire of a dragon's pet wizard would end so badly?

She took Ember out of her basket and kicked it away from her a bit. Ember went into a little nook behind her. The baby sucked on her fist and looked around like the world's cutest owl. Helene's heart glowed with love for her. *You've almost gotten me killed a hundred times since you were born,* she thought, *but I wouldn't trade you for a life a hundred years long.*

Chapter Thirteen

Diana pulled the sheet of paper out of the typewriter and handed it to Brach. She waited tensely for him to finish reading, watching his lips move as his blue eyes scanned the hastily typed page. He nodded and handed the page back, and she set it on top of the stack next to her typewriter.

"Well?" she said. "Now what?"

"Why the hell are you asking me?" he asked. "You're the creative one."

"Because I don't know what happens next." Diana stared despairingly at the paltry stack of sheets. She'd typed them front and back, a habit frowned on in the publishing world. But she didn't want to run out of paper at an inopportune time and invite the fucking Dragon back into the world. He was close. So close.

Even double-sided, the pages were too few. Only three chapters so far. Three miserable, wandering chapters. She didn't even know how the story was going to go, and now she had the added burden of bringing Helene through safely.

Her writer's heart rebelled. Her job was not to bring her characters to a happy ending. It was to write the story. If characters died, they died. That was how it had to be done.

But Helene was a live human being. Surely a human life was more important than a good story.

Wasn't it?

Well, it didn't matter much now, since Diana didn't even know what was circling in the sky toward Helene, Roger, and little Ember. She would take a break, get some dinner, and mull it over.

And maybe she'd have a little chat with their surprise visitor.

She glanced over at Francine's "one true love," a battered old man with ginger hair and the defiant scowl of a spoiled child. His name was Reuben Dark, he thought he was a wizard, and he was one of Diana's biggest mistakes.

Reuben's hands were bound with duct tape, and his hair was sopping wet with holy water. He glared at her with the sort of self-righteous indignation of someone who has been caught and knows it, but hopes that the other person doesn't. Diana flicked a silver bearing at him, and it bounced off without effect. She had already known that nothing would happen. He wasn't a werewolf or a vampire, which was a pity. It would be easier to kill him if he were.

"Why did you try to kill Helene?" she asked.

Reuben raised his chin. "You can't stop him," he said. "The dark one sees all, and he knows all your plans. He's coming for you, and he'll eat your soul."

"Gah, your dialogue is the worst," Brach groaned. "Diana, please tell me you didn't actually write this guy."

Diana looked away. "I was only a kid, and I hadn't talked to anyone in months. You could cut me a little slack if his dialogue isn't up to your Updikean standards."

Reuben kicked at her, missing by a country mile. "You didn't write me. I am my own man. I serve the dark one."

"The dark one wears many faces, and one is the face I drew forty years ago." Diana rubbed her face with both hands. "You're just a side character. You weren't supposed to stick around this long."

How could she have been so stupid? When the manifestations had first begun, she'd thought they were hallucinations. Most of her waking hours were spent in solitary confinement, so she'd assumed that loneliness and boredom was making her crazy. But when the other inmates started seeing fairies and witches in their cells at night, she should have caught on and stopped. But she hadn't, and here they were. Reuben wasn't her most dangerous or most frightening creation, but he was the one who broke her heart. He'd had so much potential.

"He can still feel pain, right?" Brach asked. He picked up an antique letter opener and held it up to the light.

"Yes, but don't you dare." Diana leaned over and cuffed his arm. "We're trying to counteract the negative energy in this place, not add to it."

"Sorry." Brach dropped the letter opener. "I think I'm just hungry."

"Me too. Why don't you go down to Sacred Grounds and get us each a turkey club. And a pumpkin spice latte. I haven't had one yet this fall, and I'm going to lose my basic bitch card."

"Will you be all right with that—person— here?" Brach stood up. Despite his visible concern, he seemed eager to be off. He shifted from foot to foot and patted his jeans, checking for his wallet.

"He can't hurt me." Diana spoke with absolute certainty.

"The Dragon King could."

"Because I wrote him that way. I suppose that means we've finally solved the existential riddle about God making a rock so big even he couldn't lift it. Off you go."

Once Brach was gone, Diana got up from the chair and sat on the floor next to Reuben. "I'm sorry," she said. "Despite what you did, I'm sorry for you. But I can't give you your life back unless you help me."

"Just write me back. Like you did the blonde bitch who killed my lady." Reuben spoke without looking at her. His gaze was fixed on some faraway point possibly not even in this world.

"You know why I can't do that. You're dead. The Knight of Stars killed you after you cursed him. Your character arc is over. The only reason you exist at all is because I brought you here."

"Then I'll just have to bring him through. If you won't send me back to my lord, I'll bring him here to me."

Diana reached out and stroked Reuben's rough cheek. He was leathery as the wings of a bat. "You don't want to do this," she whispered. "I wrote you better than this."

"What I want is irrelevant. All things serve the Book."

Diana got up and went back to her typewriter. All too true. And she was wasting valuable time. Helene and Roger had a baby to deliver.

She stopped for a break about an hour later. Helene and Roger had succeeded in evading the

Dragon King's harpy patrols, and they were now in a rough lean-to just outside the herb wife's village. The baby was finally getting fussy; Diana knew that there was only so far she could push the reader's suspension of disbelief. A mind that could accept dragons, wizards, and prophecies wasn't always a mind that could accept a baby with diaper rash who never cried.

Not that she expected to have many readers. She was writing this because Helene was right; it was the only way to undo the first book. Years of tracking down and burning old copies had been a complete waste of time. Even Ray Bradbury could have told her. Once a book was read, it could never be burned.

So she would write the sequel and finish the story the right way. And Brach would read it. Probably no one else. Would Helene read it? That depended on whether Diana could find a way to bring her back to the real world. It also depended on whether she survived her own part in it.

Her turkey sandwich had been sitting next to the typewriter all this time, and her latte was barely warmer than room temperature. Diana drank it anyway; the drink itself mattered less than the caffeine. Her sandwich was loaded with lettuce, tomato, cheese, and thousand-islands dressing, and the thick artisan bread had resisted all attempts to make it soggy. The pickle was garlicky and so crisp that it snapped apart in her mouth. Diana ate it with gusto, then she turned around to thank Brach. He wasn't in the office. Neither was Reuben.

Oh shit.

She bolted for the front of the store and clutched her thudding heart with relief. Brach and Reuben were both standing at the register, and Brach appeared to be training Reuben in its use.

His hands were freed. Diana frowned. "What are you doing with him?" If Reuben got out of the shop, she wasn't sure she could catch him again.

"Killing time, waiting for you to finish for the day," Brach said. "We're closing the shop, and then I want your help with something."

"What kind of something?" Diana didn't fully trust this. An hour ago Brach had been willing to torture this man to get what he wanted. Now they were acting like casual friends. Brach showed Reuben how to zero out the register, and Diana waited and watched in silence.

Finally Brach asked, "Can you get us into Helene's apartment?" Diana looked at Reuben, who looked away.

"Easily," she said. She needed to go up there anyway, to feed Helene's guinea pig. God only knew when Helene would be able to do it.

"I want to show him the present Francine left." Brach winked.

Diana froze. She'd told him about the sensing she'd attempted in Helene's kitchen. That flood of rage had almost killed them both, and now he wanted to introduce Reuben to it? Reuben, who had probably put the stain there in the first place?

If the rage stain upstairs was Francine's this could go very badly or very well. Reuben might go through into the other world and be consumed by the boogeyman. He might disappear forever and never trouble them again. Or he could absorb it and become even more dangerous.

Or he could join the boogeyman, add to his power, and all hell could break loose.

Diana felt mentally locked. She shifted from foot to foot and looked from Brach to Reuben. She had no idea what to do.

"Trust me," Brach said, and he winked again.

Diana nodded. She did trust Brach, and it was time to demonstrate that. She hoped that he wouldn't turn out to be the brain-dead stoner Sarah had always thought him to be. And anyway, she really did need to feed that guinea pig.

The door to Helene's upstairs apartment was locked, but Diana was friendly with the sprites that guarded it, and they let her pass. Brach and Reuben followed her closely, and she felt uneasy again. Inviting Reuben into the apartment meant that the sprites would have no power over him. She hoped like hell that Brach knew what he was doing.

Nibbles started wheeking the moment they stepped through the door. Diana felt strange entering Helene's master bedroom, a sanctuary she hadn't set foot in on her previous visits. It reeked like a petting zoo; the air was almost humid with the stench of hay, food, and animal filth. Diana backed out quickly and set to work gathering the supplies needed to clean out the pig's cage.

The bedding, vinegar spray, and other supplies were conveniently located in the adjacent bathroom. For a few minutes Brach, Reuben, and the Dragon King were completely driven out of her mind as she dumped out the urine-soaked shavings, scraped out the cage bottom, and added fresh shavings. Her eyes stung from the mingling scents of vinegar and ammonia. She hoped that the chemical combination wouldn't produce some sort of toxic reaction that could kill her. She was starting to wonder as she felt her nose hairs curl and harden.

Nibbles happily wandered around on Helene's bed while Diana cleaned. Helene had said that Nibbles was at least five years old and half-crippled, but she seemed to hobble around pretty well as far as Diana could see. One leg seemed a bit gimpy, as though she'd suffered an injury years ago, but Nibbles didn't seem to suffer from it.

Finally the cage was clean, and Diana finished by unhooking the water bottle to rinse and refill. It still had water in it, but goodness only knew when it had last been cleaned. Finally Nibbles was all set up with clean bedding, fresh pellets, and a full water bottle, and she rumbled happily when Diana put her back. Then Nibbles froze—and shrieked.

Diana screamed a little herself and clutched her chest. What was wrong? She hadn't picked her up too roughly. Nibbles' eyes were wide enough to show the whites all around, and she shrieked like a smoke alarm.

Diana started to open the cage to touch the guinea pig. That was when she heard Brach shouting curses.

She bolted into the kitchen, and before her conscious mind could take in the image her hands and mouth were reacting.

"Gentle fairies, creatures of earth and air," she babbled, pulling at the charm around her neck. "Assist me now in my hour of need. Cleanse this place of evil impurities. Rid this place of its unholy rage."

She took the dragon dust charm in her fist and held it out toward the struggling men. She stepped forward, saying, "Begone, evil one. Get thee behind me, Satan. GTFO, motherfucker." She wasn't sure yet what she was dealing with, so she recited as many rites of banishment as she could remember.

Brach was no longer cursing, but he continued to struggle. He had both arms looped through Reuben's armpits, and all of his strength was spent in keeping Reuben away from the whirling black stain in the wall. It wasn't just a smoky smudge now. It moved and roiled like a black cloud. Every couple of seconds the roiling storm took on the shape of a long, clawed hand.

"You have no power over this place, boogeyman," Diana shouted. "Get back in your book before I burn this whole place to the ground!"

The boogeyman's quiet, sibilant voice echoed in her mind, though all she could hear with her ears was a soft breeze and Reuben's whimpers. "Where is Helene?"

Diana didn't know how to answer. "She's safe. Safe from you."

"Where is she?" To Diana's shock, there was real fear in the creature's voice. "Where is Helene, gods curse you? Where?"

"She'll be back. She's helping me do something important." Diana didn't know why it was so important to placate this soulless monster, but she always listened to her gut.

The boogeyman's voice faded with the black storm. "The store has no master. It must have a master. What's to become of us?" And then it was gone.

Brach and Reuben collapsed onto the cracked linoleum floor with a thud that rattled the apartment windows. From the bedroom, Nibbles let out an inquisitive chirp.

"Trust you, huh?" Diana said, and she headed for the cabinet where Helene kept her wine. They'd polished off most of it the other day, but she thought there would be enough left for one stiff drink.

The wine was gone, but she found a bottle of tequila with an ounce or two in the bottom. Even better. Diana swigged it down, grimaced as she swallowed, then gave Brach the most self-righteous glare she could muster. "You want to explain to me what the hell you thought you were doing?" she asked. "The boogeyman was in Helene's apartment. Do you know what that means?"

"He's stronger than we thought," Brach said. He patted Reuben on the shoulder and climbed to his feet. Reuben sat on the floor and stared at the smoky stain on the wall.

"It means the barriers are breaking down!" Diana brandished the empty bottle, and they both flinched. "If the boogeyman can get out of the shop, what else could happen? I genuinely don't know."

Diana spoke authoritatively to hide the fear that clenched her stomach and bowels. She was working blind just like them, figuring things out after the fact. She hated it. Magic had rules, just like science. She had faith that the magic in Enchanted Ink followed rules like any other; she just needed to learn them. She hoped that she wouldn't learn them too late to be of any use to Helene.

"Why did you want to bring him up here?" she asked Brach, nodding at Reuben. "What did you think would happen?"

"I thought it might be a way for him to get in touch with Francine." Brach spoke to the grimy kitchen floor. Diana thought she might give it a scrub before she left tonight. "You told me about the rage stain, and I figured it must have come from Francine."

"Francine is in the boogeyman's world. Did you really think you could contact her without alerting him?" Diana shook her head and dropped the tequila bottle into the trash. It landed with a shuddering thump in the bottom of the can. She was going to need a lot more of the stuff to get through this mess.

"I didn't think he'd be able to get through up here. I thought he was locked behind his Book downstairs."

"He should have been. But he said that the store needs a master. The rules are probably cracking without Helene here, and now I don't know what he can do."

"So what does he want?" Brach sat down at the kitchen table and looked at his hands.

Diana shook her head again. "I don't know. I don't know anything. I thought I knew… but I don't."

"I miss Francine," Reuben said. He still sat on the floor, staring into the filthy corner. "I saw her, and she saw me. She reached for me, right before he came."

"I'm sorry," Brach said.

"I'm not," Diana said. "You deserved that, after the shit you pulled."

Reuben looked up at her. "I only did what you wrote," he said.

"I'm not talking about that. I'm talking about after I brought you to the real world."

Chapter Fourteen

Reuben Dark was the bastard son of a great wizard. His mother, a high-class whore with the unlikely name of Chastity, had told him from early childhood that he had magical blood and would someday do great things. "That's why I didn't flush you out like I did the others," Chastity said offhandedly. "As soon as I felt you growing, I knew you had to be the wizard's get. You won't waste your life stealing and whoring like the other bastards running around."

The other bastards were the children of Chastity's coworkers in the brothel. The whores were encouraged to take preventative measures, but in the event that it failed the management staff was good about supplying adequate care and paid time off for maternity. That was why The Lord's Harem was the highest quality brothel in the business, and why it could afford the loveliest and cleanest whores in the Walled Kingdom. Chastity was the most beautiful of them all, with her cat-green eyes and fiery hair, and her clients were titillated by her swollen breasts and belly during her pregnancy. What also helped her bottom line was the rumor that women with red hair had witch's blood. It gave the encounter a sense of danger.

The children were well cared for while they were small and easy to feed, but they were never expected to amount to much. "Whores breed what whores is," one fat old merchant was overheard to say, to general agreement. It was understood by most, including the working girls themselves, that their children would grow up to pick pockets, cheat the gullible, and ultimately end up in a brothel themselves, regardless of gender.

But Chastity had determined that this would not be her son's future. An actual wizard had visited her, an old man in long black robes that sparkled like hidden stars. He'd come specifically for the "red-haired temptress," and he'd kept her busy until daybreak. Weeks later, when her red flower failed to bloom, she'd known instantly that this child was his. Only a wizard's seed could be powerful enough to bypass the layers of protection Chastity kept in place. Ever since her third (and hopefully last) abortion, she left nothing to chance. This child was meant to be.

When Reuben was nine years old, she serviced an old man with a club foot and significant bedroom difficulties. It took hours of expert care to bring the liaison to a successful conclusion, but the old man's gratitude made her sore jaw worth it. In addition to the standard brothel fee he offered her a generous private stipend, which she declined. "I have no need of money for myself," she said between sips of healing fruit juice, "but a future for my son—that is something that money cannot buy."

The banker got the hint. A week later Reuben was in a carriage headed to an apprenticeship in Ward City with a new identity as the banker's adopted ward and something he'd never had before: a last name. Reuben the Whore's Bastard was now Reuben Dark. Mr. Dark had only two caveats on his generosity: that Reuben be both silent and obedient at all times, and that Chastity keep her schedule open for his visits. Chastity sighed, rubbed her jaw, and agreed. Reuben did as well. He was a quiet lad by nature, so keeping silent in the face of a new world and strange people was an easy promise to keep.

Reuben moved in with the Darks' housemaid, a chubby little woman with a round face and an abiding hatred of Lady Dark. Missy liked to steal her ladyship's private belongings and then return them when the lady raised a fuss over their disappearance. It wasn't always something valuable; Reuben once watched Lady Dark turn the household inside out over a missing peacock feather. It wasn't money that Missy was after, but the lady's humiliation.

Reuben watched Missy carefully. He thought that this chubby, invisible person could teach him more than all the counting lessons in the world. She stole things as a lark and passed it off to Reuben as a funny joke, but he saw the sternness behind her eyes when she slipped a hand mirror or fur slipper into her pocket. These were not pranks, Reuben felt, but something more serious in Missy's mind. This was a campaign.

Missy was also an excellent judge of character, and by watching her Reuben was able to pick out the little tics and hints that people were not all that they appeared. A twinkle-eyed, fawning older woman visited Lady Dark once and brought Reuben a box of sweets. Missy whispered to him later that the old lady had a murderer's aura, and it was true that her first husband had died under peculiar circumstances. Reuben gave the sweets to Lady Dark's children, who gobbled them eagerly without so much as a thank-you.

All told, Reuben lived with the banker for three years. He learned sums and counting, and he became a trusted employee of the bank after only two years. He only stole small amounts of money, and Mr. Dark always expected and allowed for it. He considered it pocket money for the boy. Considering Reuben's parentage, Mr. Dark thought it a miracle that the child wasn't already sexually deviant. His relief on this score made him magnanimous with funds.

Reuben enjoyed the time he spent in the Dark household, but he never felt satisfied. Part of it was the way they all treated him; it was generally assumed that he was Mr. Dark's bastard, so they paid him the contemptuous deference allotted to a child who could dream of greatness but would never be any better than he was. It was a step up from being treated like the fatherless child of a whore, so he didn't like to complain even inwardly. He knew he needed to be grateful for this opportunity, and he was. But all the same, he felt awkward and out of place among their fancy dishes and sneering kindness.

The root of his dissatisfaction was in the memory of his mother's words. He was the son of a wizard and destined for a magical future. There was nothing magical about learning to count ten pennies and pocket the eleventh. Who was his father? Where had he gone? Did he know Reuben existed, and if so would be come looking for him someday?

These questions kept Reuben's mind occupied on long, boring days at his counting desk, and in the wee hours of the night when he could not sleep. At last he decided that he'd had enough of high quality people and their high quality but boring lives. He spent a few weeks gathering and hoarding food and money, and he slipped away one dark night during a thunderstorm. The pounding rain and wind concealed the sound of his departure out his bedroom window, and when Dark's guard dogs barked at him at the gate, everyone assumed that they were barking at the storm and ignored them.

The temperature was mild in spite of the driving rain, and Reuben was comfortable in his oiled cloak. He carried a sack of apples, cheese, and other portable foodstuffs, and at the bottom the sack was filled with coins. Reuben didn't want to draw attention to himself by demonstrating wealth, but a bedraggled youth paying for bread in pennies would draw no attention.

The Dark family made only a token attempt to find him. The banker was relieved to see him go; he'd had misgivings from the start about letting a whore's son apprentice in his business, and the lad's disappearance meant that if his blood did eventually manifest, the trouble would be elsewhere. His wife was easier in his mind as well. She knew he had other lovers—as did she—but she was still furious about having to feed and provide for the evidence.

The only person who sincerely missed him was Missy. She'd come to love the boy and enjoy the time they spent together, cleaning up after the Darks and stealing their belongings. She disappeared suddenly one afternoon and was found floating in the Ward River three days later.

Reuben left the city of Ward and headed east, toward the isles. The Eastern Isles seemed the likeliest spot in the Kingdoms for a wizard to make his home. Reuben's counting tutor, a brown-eyed little man named Jet, had told him all about the Eastern Isles. They were wild, secluded islands full of strange trees and stranger animals. The foliage was so beautiful and exotic that the birds and insects there were dressed in flaming colors as camouflage. The oceans moved constantly, bringing magic, food, and wonders to the inhabitants. It was so hot there that the people rarely wore clothes, and they regarded formal dress as a foolish waste of resources.

Reuben headed in that direction with the hope of finding a clue to his supposed wizardly parentage, but he also thought that if he didn't find it, he could still find a home among the people of the Eastern Isles. They sounded like his kind of people. His mother had always sneered at high class ladies with gloves and corsets and untouchable hair. "Of course your man will come to someone like us," he'd heard her say to a friend, "if they can't get at the goods inside your own dress." Reuben wasn't sure she was right—farmers and beggars visited whores as often as nobles—but he shared her wondering contempt at many of the customs of the upper class. Many of them, he felt, would vanish in a puff of smoke within a week of honest work.

He travelled mostly by day, resting by night in barns and lean-tos. When he ran out of his saved food and money, he bartered with physical labor. He wasn't skilled, but one didn't need to be a born farmer to push carts, haul water, or hold a pig steady for the knife. He lived on whatever the farmers and traders could spare, usually corn or potatoes or a bit of dried meat. Reuben accepted what was offered and never argued, even when it seemed to him that they could have spared more. But he remembered the less-generous farmers, and he made a note of their location.

The cool spring weather grew warmer, and the air grew moist and heavy. Just when it was about to get unpleasant, he woke up to a cool morning breeze that smelled like salt. He was getting close to the ocean. He picked up his pace, anxious to be rid of the dry, boring mainland. He wanted to see the bright birds and the naked people. Did nipples tan or burn in the sun?

But fate had other plans for him, and it manifested in the shape of the most terrifying being Reuben could have imagined.

He spent a warm early summer night in the shelter of a thick-barked tree with wide spreading branches and succulent leaves the size of dinner plates. He had never seen a tree like this before, and he took it as a sign that he really was about to enter a beautiful new world. After a pauper's meal of potatoes and bread, he covered himself with his cloak and fell asleep with a smile on his face.

He was awakened in the early hours before dawn by a faint rumble, like distant thunder. He crawled out of his shelter, looking for rain. What he saw made him literally piss himself.

The enormous black dragon looked down at him with a faint gleam in its catlike golden eyes. Its voice was rough but intelligible as it growled, "So you're the one they told me about. So far I'm not impressed."

The smell of piss was hot and wet in Reuben's nostrils, and he swallowed a lump in his throat. He did not try to speak. If he spoke it would come out as a blubber, and he couldn't face that. Bad enough he was about to die with piss running down his leg; he didn't want to die crying too.

"If I wanted you dead, you would be," the dragon growled. "Stop your sniveling."

Even through his fear Reuben heard the logic in its words. He swallowed again and took a shuddering breath. "Do—do you know any wizards?" he stammered. "Did one send you?"

The dragon lowered its great horned head and cocked a golden eye at him. "Wizard, eh?" it rumbled. "Like this?" And it vanished. In its place was an old man with a magnificent white beard and sparkling black robes.

Reuben had never seen his father of course, but Chastity had described him in detail many times during the long daylight hours before her working shift began. All of those details came rushing back to him now.

His beard glinted like crystals where the sun touched. Bushy white eyebrows over piercing blue eyes. Chastity had rhapsodized over those eyes often enough that meeting them now brought a prickle of recognition. His jet-black robes were stitched with silvery stones that made them glitter in the sunlight. Reuben chose not to think about the rest of Chastity's description, the verification of which would require more intimacy than Reuben felt comfortable with. The wizard smiled, exposing the white, even teeth of a noble.

"Father?" Reuben said. He cocked his head, and the wizard's smile widened.

"The scrying pond told me that my son was coming to seek me out," the wizard said. His voice was gentle and cultured. "I couldn't believe it until I saw for myself."

"Mother was right," Reuben said. "My magical destiny finally came back for me."

"In a manner of speaking." The wizard blinked, and his blue eyes turned golden. Then he blinked again, and they were back to blue.

"Is the dragon your messenger?" Reuben asked. "Did you ride him?"

"Ah, no." The wizard vanished, and once again the dragon loomed over him. It clenched its talons, tearing furrows into the earth. Reuben gulped and stared up into enormous blue eyes. Finally, the truth dawned on him.

"Mother," he whispered. "What did you do?"

"Your mother was an exceptional woman," the dragon growled. "You should be proud. What remains to be seen is whether I should be proud of you. Come." It reached out and curled its talons around Reuben's body. "We're going for a ride."

****

Chastity heard of Reuben's disappearance on Mr. Dark's last visit. "My men followed his trail to a cave near the sea, and after that all trace of him vanished. Nearby there were scorch marks on the ground, and several trees were snapped in half—as though an enormous monster had passed."

Chastity kept it together for the sake of professionalism, but after Dark had left she went into hysterics. She and the other whores hired a trio of mercenaries to search for Reuben, but their search ended at the same cold trail.

She couldn't avoid the reality. The son she'd thought would grow up to a wonderful destiny had been hunted and killed by some enormous monster. The Walled Kingdom was supposed to keep them all safe from such predation, but clearly it had failed.

Chastity retired from the whorehouse soon after that, and it was rumored that she died of grief in the streets of Ward City.

Chapter Fifteen

Diana and the two men sat around the rickety Formica table in Helene's kitchen. They drank and stared at each other. Brach had volunteered to go out for another bottle of tequila, no doubt to both atone for and briefly escape Diana's fury. When he'd returned, she'd grabbed three glasses and sat down without a word. Now they drank silently, and stared.

"How on earth did you convince this idiot to let you try to reach Francine in the boogeyman's realm?" Diana demanded of Reuben. "This has got to be one of the dumbest plot twists I've ever heard."

"Why did you let me out?" Reuben returned. "Why did you bring me to this world? You knew from the start that I'm loyal to the one true king. You had to know that I would protect the Book at all costs. You yell at me for all the terrible things I've done, but you were the one who brought me here, so who's really responsible?"

Diana dropped her eyes to her tequila glass. It had a blue unicorn on it. "I thought I could fix you," she mumbled. "You were a good guy. You just needed to get in touch with your human side. I thought getting you away from the Dragon King would help. Also—I was lonely."

Had she ever been. So much time spent in solitary during her ten years in prison. Even masturbating was a crime in there. Her only solace had been her book.

"I'm not human," Reuben said softly. "You should know that better than anyone."

Diana sighed and took another sip. "I do now."

Finally, when the bottle was half-empty and Diana was feeling a bit calmer, Reuben said, "I'm sorry."

She couldn't say that it was all right, so Diana settled for, "I know. We are going to try to get her out of here."

"I know." There was a long, heavy silence. Then he asked, "So why did you bring me here? Really?"

She poured herself another inch and downed it before replying. "Same reason I did everything when I was twenty years old. I was pissed off. I knew I could. And I felt like it."

"But you're mad at me for being selfish and stupid?"

He had a point, and Diana reverted her attention to the blue unicorn on her glass. There were little white ducks around it. She wondered if anyone had ever written a horror story about cute ducks.

In truth, she hadn't really known what she was doing when she'd written Reuben into the real world. There had been hints of what was to come when the ghostly witches and medieval soldiers had appeared to wander through the halls of the prison. Then, after *Imprisonment of Hope* had defied all odds and made it to print, she'd started dreaming about the Dragon King. Powerful, sexy dreams that still made her shudder to remember. But that lonely day, just a year before making parole, she'd let her imagination take over, and she'd—written. Scribbled it all out on paper, and then watched Reuben casually stroll into her cell and smile at her. Even then, she'd thought it was a hallucination. He seemed to appear and disappear like a dream, until she'd gotten paroled.

Her first night in her new apartment, he'd appeared one last time. And stayed. And here he remained. Working for her, and working against her. Bastard son of the Dragon King.

Had she known what she was doing, when she'd summoned him? Night after night, when she'd prayed for him to be real, had she known that it could actually happen? It didn't matter now. What mattered was that it was done, and the magic she'd thought she'd harnessed was wildly out of control.

"We need to get Helene back," Brach said. His cheeks were flushed with drink, and his blue eyes were moist.

"I know. I wish I knew how." Diana closed her eyes. The room was swaying gently.

"You brought me out," Reuben said, putting his head down on the table.

"Yes, but if I do it like that, she'll still be poisoned by the dragon dust. Asshole. I'm going to bed." Diana stood up carefully and wandered in the general direction of Helene's bedroom. She made it as far as the living room couch and sat down. "Forget the bed. Too tired. I'm going to couch." She lay down and closed her eyes.

Her eyes darted open, and suddenly she was wide awake and sober. That meant she was dreaming again. *Shit. Please don't let it be one of those dreams,* she thought.

She caught a whiff of sulfur, and her heart raced. But the apartment was dark and quiet. There was no sign of Brach or Reuben. Or Reuben's father.

"Hey." Diana turned to face a good-looking man of about thirty, with shaggy hair and sleeve tattoos up both arms. His bristly face was thin, and there were dark circles under his blue eyes.

"You must be Christopher," Diana said at last.

"In the flesh. Not really. Your boyfriend's really stirred up some shit, you know that? The big guy is pissed." Christopher's tone was nonchalant, but Diana saw the tension in his jaw and in his tightened fists.

"I'm sorry," Diana said. "I never should have let them in here. I should have known what they would try."

Christopher shrugged. "At least the dragon didn't find his way in. That's what the big guy is really afraid of. It shouldn't be possible, but a lot of this shit isn't possible. I don't even know what's real anymore."

"I know how that feels. Listen, are you here looking for Helene? Do you know what happened to her?"

"Yes. And no." Christopher's eyes focused on her like a beam.

Diana explained, and Christopher took it better than she'd expected. "Well," he said, "once your existence has reached a certain level of fucked up, what's a few more kicks in the ass, huh? Now I see what the big guy was so worked up about."

"You seem to understand this boogeyman better than I do. What can you tell me about his world?"

Vellichor

Christopher again focused his brilliant blue eyes on her, as though probing for information. Then he took a deep breath and began.

****

Christopher barely remembered the day of his capture. He'd been bored to death but unwilling to leave Helene; that much he did remember. She'd been spending too much time alone here, and it was making her see and think things that weren't real. That couldn't be real. She said that she knew that, that it was just her mind playing tricks and making up stories to entertain her, but she always said it with a nervous, distracted smile. And she never seemed to meet his eyes when she said it.

He knew better than anyone that her past was filled with incidents like this, where she would describe a dream or a story and think that it had actually happened. But aside from her odd quirks about the "characters" living in the shop, she'd seemed completely rational and normal. So he'd let it go and ignored when she would stare at a particular corner of the shop or speak to someone he couldn't see. He could have kicked himself for that now.

Now, when he looked back on the day that the boogeyman took him, it was like trying to remember a dream. The only real world now was the world of the Book. It worried him sometimes to think that way, since he knew in his conscious logical mind that the Book was the fantasy and the shop was reality. But it was so hard to tell the difference. There was no day or night where he was, nothing but pages and words and long, reaching claws.

His voice went strange and wondering as he tried to describe it to Diana. "The ground isn't there. You're walking on nothing. Not invisible, not clear, just not there at all. But it's smooth under your feet, like you're walking on paper. And the pages are all around you. They stretch all the way up into the sky, only there is no sky. Just more pages. The whole world is book pages. Black printing on white paper. And you have to be careful of the words."

"The words? Why?" Diana clamped her hands together on her lap. The young man's eyes looked so dark and haunted. Hungry. He looked like he was starving. She looked away from his eyes.

"They don't do anything until you read them. But then they come alive. Whatever you read in there becomes real, even if you don't understand what you're reading. And if you read it out loud—I did it once, because the big guy told me not to. I only did it once. The story took me over. I lived it. And the things I saw... they took a long time to die."

Diana closed her eyes briefly, and when she opened them Christopher was looking at her. "He feeds on fear." His voice was low and urgent. "That's why he takes us. He drives us to terror, then he feeds. Over and over again. I can't sleep. There's no darkness, no night. Just the bright. White. Pages. Just the Book."

"I'm so sorry," Diana said. Her heart was thudding in her chest. Helene had never told her any of this. Maybe she didn't know. "I'll find a way to get you out of there." A glimmer of an idea twinkled in her mind. "I might know a way. I want to save you and Helene both."

"I miss her. Do you think she's all right?"

"Yes, I do." She leaned over and squeezed Christopher's hand. It was cold as marble. "And I'm going to find a way to fix all this, bring the wild magic under control."

Christopher met her eyes one last time. "I have to go. He's looking for me. Goodbye."

Diana opened her eyes with a sick groan. Now she was truly awake, and she wished she wasn't. Before she'd even moved, it was as if a bolt of lightning was stabbing her through the left eye, and her stomach felt like she'd swallowed a lead ball.

The Dragon King. The boogeyman. Two sides of the same dark coin. Fuck them both. Diana needed an energy drink and about a gallon of water. She sat up slowly and rubbed her head. When would she remember that she couldn't drink like a kid anymore?

There was a glass of water and a pair of aspirin on the coffee table in front of her. Diana's eyebrows rose. Brach was more of a gentleman than she remembered. The gesture more than the medicine itself eased her sore head a trifle and lifted her spirits a bit more. Slowly she made her way downstairs to the shop.

The clock on the wall behind the register said nine o'clock. The store didn't open for another hour, and there was no sign of Brach or Reuben. Her head still hurt, and she wasn't in the mood to hear voices, so the quiet suited her.

The view outside the shop was grey with drizzling rain. Diana slowly unlocked the front door and stepped out into the wet.

The air was warm and humid, but the rain dripped down was cold as a corpse. Diana lifted her face and felt the cold darts strike her face, ears, and neck. She opened her mouth and tasted of the grey sky. Water is life, she thought dreamily. Her hangover was fading.

The warm air and cold rain made her feel reckless and young again. What the hell. Acting like a rational adult hadn't done her much good up until now. "Apepapophis," she said to the sky. "Come to me. You are a man, and I am a woman. I wish to palaver, woman to man."

"As you wish, my love." A pale man of about her age, with brilliant blue eyes and a sparkling white beard, stood on the wet sidewalk beside her. Diana smelled sulfur, and she leaned away a bit. The fat raindrops never touched his black suit jacket. Tiny gems sewn into the fabric made his suit seem to glitter in the dim light.

"Don't call me that," she said.

"But you are." Apep's tone was reverent. "You are my mother, my lover, and my everything. Let's go inside the shop and palaver, as you wish."

"Nice try." Diana stepped away and forked the sign of the evil eye at him. He gritted his teeth and hissed like a disappointed vampire. "You go into the shop, you pass the barrier and manifest in your true form. That's not happening. We'll talk out here."

"In front of the whole mortal world?" Apep looked around. There was nobody visible on the street, but there could be eyes all around, behind the windows of the shops and houses. They would be engaged in their own affairs, but might there not be one or two curious faces turned in their direction? Diana knew he was right. She couldn't risk letting the world see him, especially since she wasn't sure what his powers were, in mortal form.

"We'll go for coffee." What could be more normal and boring than that? Diana stalked away down the street, and Apep followed. Her sandal slipped on the wet cement, and she caught herself quickly. In an instant Apep was at her side and tried to take her arm. In a heartbeat her hangover was back with a vengeance.

"Have a care, my love," he murmured, and Diana shook him off with an oath.

The rain fell thicker, pounding on her head and shoulders like a cold shower. The empty street gleamed with puddles in the dim morning light, and Diana sniffed away a droplet of rain that hung from her nose.

The door into Sacred Grounds seemed heavier than usual, and Diana muttered an incantation to ease the stress on her aching head. When Apep followed her in, he glared at her. "You did this on purpose!"

"Did what?" At first she thought he was talking about her lightening the door. Then she noticed the young woman at the register staring at them. The girl's hair was blonde streaked with sky-blue, and her eyes were the same shade of blue. And those eyes were fixed on Apep without blinking.

"Who is that girl?" Apep muttered. "Why is she staring at me? And for the devil's sake, why am I suddenly mortal?"

"Are you really?" Diana reached out and touched Apep's arm. Under the glistening suit jacket, he felt warm and alive and mammalian. "You're human! I can't feel your scales at all."

"No shit." Apep spoke through gritted teeth. Even, smooth, mortal teeth. "Now who is she? And how does she recognize me?"

There appeared to be a look of dawning recognition on the young barista's face, but Diana had no idea how to answer the rest of his question. "That's Rachel. Her parents own this coffee shop. Her dad used to be a priest."

Apep relaxed. "That's it, then. We're on holy ground. I'll return to my normal self once we leave." He breathed a heavy sigh. "Smart of you to bring me here. I wouldn't think you were clever enough."

Diana wasn't about to admit that it was just a lucky break, so she led him to the counter in silence. Rachel barely took her eyes off Apep as she took Diana's order for two caramel lattes and two cranberry muffins. Her fingers flew over the keyboard on the register as though of their own accord. Diana wasn't sure that she even blinked once during the exchange.

After paying for their snacks Diana led Apep to the most secluded table in the shop. Sadly the place had no booths, but at least it was mostly empty this morning except for a middle aged woman with thick dark glasses and a German Shepherd dog under her table. The blind woman drank a hot coffee and fiddled with what looked like a smart phone. Could blind people use that type of phone? Maybe there was a special app for people with sight difficulties. And maybe Diana was people watching instead of focusing on the situation sitting across from her.

"So why did you summon me?" Apep asked, looking down at his smooth, fleshy hands. "After all this time?"

Vellichor

"I wasn't expecting you to answer," Diana said. "You didn't last time."

Diana had summoned the Dragon King using his true name. Answering that call meant giving up most of his power and entering the world under her control. Unless he found a way into Enchanted Ink, where there was enough wild magic to break the rope of Fenris that bound him in this world.

Back in her misspent youth, before she knew what she was really doing, Diana had summoned him a dozen times. Largely, she was ashamed to remember, for sex. She hadn't been stupid enough to wish him real as she had Reuben, but summoning an evil dragon to use as a sex toy was plenty stupid enough. She'd always been an idiot when it came to her womanhood. But when people who read her books started having nightmares, when spontaneous fires had erupted in half a dozen homes, she'd put a stop to it.

That was when she'd started burning the books.

"I told you once that I love you," Apep said. "Why don't you believe me?"

"Because you don't love anyone. Whenever you manifest in this world, you spread hatred and lies and war. You don't even love your son; you just use him as a cat's paw. I ought to know. I wrote you that way. But now I'm going to put an end to it."

"You can't stop a story once it's been written. You should know that by now."

"No, but I can write a new one. A better one."

Apep froze, and Diana relished the look of uncertainty on his bearded face. Their coffees arrived before he could respond, and Diana took her first sip in complete satisfaction.

"You can't change what happened," he said. His voice was weak. As weak as that of a scared, stupid twenty-year-old who had just made the biggest mistake of her life.

"No, but I can change what will happen." Diana took another sip of coffee. "Apepapophis, you are dismissed from this mortal plane."

When she looked up from her coffee, the bearded man was gone. So was the coffee.

Chapter Sixteen

When Diana got back, the bookstore was already open. Brach stood at the front register, chatting with a dirty-faced boy child in a porkpie hat. The boy waved at Diana and skipped away, towards the back of the shop.

"That's the children's section back there, right?" Diana said to Brach. She leaned on the counter. "Not classic literature?"

"Ollie likes the talking animals back there," Brach said. "He says his own section is too dusty. I don't think he means the condition of the books."

"I agree with him." Diana had never been a fan of the classics, though she had found a few rare gems that weren't terrible. Still, she always felt suspicious of people who claimed to read Dickens or Austin for fun. "Where's Reuben?"

Brach jerked his head. "In the office, reading your book."

Diana felt uneasy about that. The book was so important, and Reuben was not trustworthy. And she had no backup copy. The fragile pages sitting on the desk were all of the story.

But she had one more question. "Did he ever explain exactly what his relationship was to Francine?"

"He met her at the party that night, and he claims that it was love at first sight. He never meant for her to die in the fire."

"He had the last book. The original copy that I've been trying to destroy. He brought it here and gave it to Helene, to read."

"He wanted to ask the Dragon King to bring Francine back to the living world."

"He's delusional. The King has no power over the realm of the dead."

"Hope springs eternal, I guess." Brach nodded at a young woman in a flannel shirt and black-rimmed glasses, who walked in like a pilgrim at Mecca. God bless hipsters, Diana thought as she went into the office. Making used book stores trendy.

To her relief Reuben was only sitting at the typewriter, doing nothing more ominous than reading the pages stacked next to it. She hadn't thought seriously that he would do anything to the book—he rarely did anything dangerous or destructive without explicit instruction from his father—but he was unpredictable and irrational. Hence their current difficulties.

"So that's how you saved Helene," he said, putting down the last page.

"She wasn't the one who exorcised Francine, you know." Diana sat down on a nearby stool. "It was my spell, and my idea."

"I know. But I can't hurt you."

"You're a sniveling little wyrm of a man."

Reuben looked up and bared his teeth at her. His incisors were a bit pointed and longer than average. It gave his gingery face a feral appearance. "You're just like God, you know that? Create an imperfect character and then get pissed off that he's not perfect."

He was absolutely right, which made Diana even more angry. After joining forces with his father, he had betrayed and murdered the entire Dark family, right down to the chambermaid's suckling child. In a chapter *she* had written. It was that betrayal that had triggered his mother's suicide, according to rumor. Chastity had been heartbroken to hear of how her special, beloved son had turned out, and she had taken her own life.

"I need to go back to work," she said. "Go make yourself useful."

"I wasn't born to be useful. I was born to greatness."

More of that dreadful dialogue. It made Diana cringe at her younger self. As she nudged him out of the way to reach the typewriter, he added, "You smell like a locker room. When did you last shower?"

It hadn't been more than a day or two, but she was probably sweating out yesterday's tequila. "Fuck off," she said, and she sat down with a heavy thud. She'd be sure to take a shower before inviting Brach back to her room again.

She loaded a fresh sheet of paper into the typewriter and breathed a deep sigh. The paper was so pure, so white. But nothing perfect ever lasted, even in stories. She placed her fingers in the home key position (thank you, Ms. Adee) steeled her frayed nerves, and got to work.

****

When Francine awoke, the first sense that came back to her was smell. She smelled paper, old paper, like the bookstore she'd haunted for so many years. But this was so much stronger. She coughed lightly and sat up.

The walls were close around her. She felt like she could touch them both with her fingertips, but when she reached out they skated away. The walls were stark white, almost glowing, and covered with huge black words. The contrast—black words, white walls—made her vision dance, and she closed her eyes.

A large, warm hand gripped her upper arm. A man's voice whispered, "Don't look at the words."

Francine opened her eyes and looked into a familiar face. It was Helene's man friend, gaunt and shaggy as though he'd been living rough. His eyes were large and blue and earnest. "Don't read the words," he repeated. "They want you to read them. It makes things happen."

"What kind of things?" she asked. She glanced at the nearest line of text. Gaunt arms reached for her, and she could see the dead flesh peeling away…

"That kind!" Christopher shouted. He grabbed her arm in both hands and yanked her to her feet. Francine cringed at his touch, though it didn't hurt. She had been dead too long to feel physical pain. But apparently she could still feel fear, because she felt her heart thudding in her chest, constricting her throat, as the rotting, moaning, undead thing materialized out of the words and lurched towards them. She couldn't scream; all she could do was follow Christopher and think, *Please don't touch me, please don't, those horrible hands, flesh rotting and peeling off those horrid bones…*

Vellichor

And sneaking in behind the fear was an odd, selfish question. What do my hands look like now? Thirty years. How much of my bones are exposed?

But Christopher kept her moving, and eventually they left the lurching corpse behind. They slowed to a walk, and Christopher finally let go of her arm.

She said, "You've been here all this time. This is what the inside of the boogeyman's Book looks like, isn't it?"

"Yes." Christopher rubbed his face with both hands. "He feeds on fear. We're like—his cows. He milks us for fear."

It was hard to look around without reading more than a word or two. Francine settled for looking down at her feet. They seemed to stand on nothing. She tapped her foot, and there was no sound. But the surface seemed firm enough. Maybe she was standing on invisible paper.

"How can you stand this?" she whispered. "I would go crazy."

"The big guy would love that. He likes madness almost as much as he likes fear. But there are a few safe places. I'll show you the title page. And sometimes, if you're careful and quick, you can find holes in the pages where you can sneak back to the real world. But not really, because people can only see you when they're asleep. And he'll always catch you and bring you back. Then he punishes you."

"Punishes me how?" Francine was dead. What could he threaten her with?

Christopher shook his head. "He's the boogeyman. He was in your closet when you were a little girl. Under your crib when you were a baby. He knows everything you're afraid of. And it's all here, in the Book."

Francine's body hardened with gooseflesh. Christopher nodded and squeezed her shoulder in sympathy. "I know. Come on, I'll show you the title page. It's safer there."

****

There was no time here in the Book. No day or night or afternoon tea. Just endless white walls and crawling black words. Francine avoided looking at the words as much as possible, but it wasn't easy. She never got tired or footsore, but she did get bored. Sooner or later her mind would wander, her eyes would drift away from her feet, and within moments some horrifying creature was looming over her or seizing her ankle. It was a tiresome existence, and she wondered how Christopher had kept his sanity for so long.

The holes in the paper helped. They looked like little black storms, swirling dark masses no bigger than a basketball. Through them she could slip away into the shop for a moment or two and catch her breath. Nobody could see her on the other side, but Francine was used to that. She did manage to speak briefly to Helene while she slept, and it must have done some good because the old lady Diana finally got to work on the damn book.

But Christopher hadn't been kidding when he said that the boogeyman would punish her. After each excursion she came back to the Book to face some horrible memory from her childhood. The first time was the uncle who had hugged her at the

Christmas party and squeezed her butt cheek. She had been six.

The nightmares went downhill from there. But still she looked for ways out of the Book, as much out of contrariness as anything. She hoped that her constant defiance was at least annoying the boogeyman, though she had no way of knowing.

Then, a bit later—Francine had no way of knowing how much later—something changed. The bright whiteness of her prison flared, blinding her. Then it dimmed to nearly total darkness, almost obscuring the words. Francine started to squint at them, trying to make them out, before she caught herself. Then the whiteness returned, and all was as it had been.

"What happened?" she asked Christopher.

He shook his head. "I don't know. But do you feel weird? Like something is off-balance?"

Francine shifted from one foot to another and nodded. She did feel a little off-kilter. As though the floor beneath her feet was tilted slightly. Or the wobbly feeling one got after getting off a very long elevator ride.

"I'll ask the big guy," he said.

"You're going to talk to him?" Francine clasped her hands together. The boogeyman rarely manifested before them; Christopher thought that he was putting all of his focus on the Dragon King, who lurked in his own book nearby. All Francine knew was that the boogeyman was terrifying, and she was happy to see as little of them as possible.

Christopher took a deep breath, lifted his head, and shouted, "Yo! Asshole!"

A swirling black cloak whipped past their faces, and a familiar voice spoke in their ears. "I've no time for your foolishness now. The shop has lost its anchor. The wild magic is breaking down, and anything could happen. Where the devil is Helene?"

And then he was gone.

They stood in blank silence for an immeasurable amount of time. Finally Christopher said, "That was unexpected."

"Did he say the ship or the shop?" Francine asked. There was a story in this Book about a haunted steamliner, but she didn't think a short story that hadn't been read in years could upset the boogeyman so badly.

"He said the shop has lost its anchor." Christopher scratched his scruffy beard. There was no time, no sleep, and no hunger here in the Book, but his beard still grew, loose and scraggy. Probably only because he thought it should. Or because Helene thought it should.

"Enchanted Ink has an anchor?" This made no sense at all to Francine.

"I think he means Helene. Your boyfriend tried to kill her, and Diana saved her by writing her into her new book. Maybe Helene knows about this anchor and how it works, the big man seems to think she would."

He'd also said something else, something that mattered a lot more to Francine than that stuffy blonde bitch. "He also said something about wild magic. He said anything could happen. Does that mean that we could escape?"

"Maybe." Christopher looked around doubtfully. "I don't see any holes, though."

Vellichor

Francine stomped her foot on the nonexistent ground. "Wild magic means there aren't any rules! It's loose power, like a nuclear spill. Anything could happen, he said. If there's wild magic spilling through the books, then we could walk right out of here."

****

Now how did she know that? She didn't remember who had told her. Maybe she'd read it somewhere, though she had never been much of a reader.

"I don't know." Christopher scratched his beard again. "It doesn't seem safe. What if we run into something even worse than what we're running from in here?"

Francine rolled her eyes and stamped her foot again. Something about this skinny little man made her feel about ten years old. "You are such an old woman! Don't you want to see Helene again?"

"Helene's not there. The big guy just said—"

"Well I want to get back to Reuben! Nothing else matters but being with him! So I don't care what you do, but I'm going back to the shop!"

She didn't say home. Enchanted Ink had never felt like home to her, but right now it was where Reuben was, and that was all that mattered. He was her home, always had been.

Francine turned away, ignoring Christopher's worried expression. She faced the page and stared at the white space between the words. That was where the holes always appeared, and that was where her exit would appear now. She would make it happen.

This time the boogeyman would not be able to pull her back. She was leaving this horrible place, and she would never be dragged back into this terrible Book. Christopher could stay here and whine about poor pathetic Helene. Francine was going to take charge of her own existence for once.

She glared at the white space between the words blackness and horror. She ignored them. The Book had no power over her anymore. She was going back to find her one true love. Reuben was waiting for her at the shop. She would not let him down.

Open up! she thought impatiently. Paper, tear open. Let me through. I'm going.

"I don't like this," Christopher said behind her left shoulder.

A cold trickle of unease teased her stomach, but she ignored it. Christopher was trying to get to her, infect her with his whiny paranoia. The boogeyman ruled by fear. Francine would not be ruled by anyone. Not anymore.

"Open up," she muttered aloud.

And slowly, miraculously, the white space widened. A black vertical line appeared and shivered into a thin crack. The crack spread slightly, making a black space just wide enough for a child or a very slender woman to squeeze through.

Christopher touched her arm. "Francine. I've got a bad feeling about this. Please."

His voice was low and urgent. The voice of a trained psychologist trying to talk a jumper back from the ledge. Francine paused and looked at him. His face was thinner and more haggard than ever. He looked like he'd aged ten years in thirty seconds.

He really was afraid. Francine hesitated one last time.

Vellichor

But then she thought of Reuben. Reuben wasn't afraid of anyone. He had told her, that fateful night at the party, about his great destiny. At the time she'd thought that he was just making up a wild story to amuse her, but her perception had widened since her death.

"I'm leaving now," she said clearly, and she turned toward the crack.

"Yo! Asshole!" Christopher cried into the pale sky.

"You son of a bitch," Francine said, and she dashed for the opening. The black slit loomed close and large, and she shoved her body through the gap as hard as she could. Christopher did not try to restrain her. Maybe he knew that as a ghost, she couldn't be touched if she didn't want to be. Or maybe he didn't want to get too close to the rip in the paper.

It was an effort to press herself through, but Francine could smell coffee and dust in the darkness on the other side. She kicked and shoved her way in. She was going home to Reuben. He was waiting for her.

At last she burst through the gap. She was free.

The darkness was silent. She couldn't smell coffee and old books anymore. This was unexpected. How could she find her way? She looked around, but Christopher and the Book were gone. She was surrounded by featureless darkness.

She would find a way. Love would always win. *Reuben,* she thought. *My one true love.* She thought of ginger hair, big blue eyes with flecks of gold in them. *My darling Reuben.*

From the moment they'd met she'd felt like she'd known him forever. He'd told her his mother was a whore, and she'd laughed and said, "Yeah mine is no prize either." It had taken Francine a while to realize that he'd meant a literal prostitute. Apparently a really hot piece, like the strippers out in Vegas. Francine was a little jealous. She barely remembered her own mother.

I wonder what his father looked like, she thought. She started walking through the dark and tried to imagine it. Obviously he wasn't a literal dragon, if he had slept with a prostitute. Did he have red hair like Reuben's?

I'd like to meet him. I'd thank him for making Reuben. He's just so perfect, she mused.

Bright golden eyes opened in the darkness in front of her. Francine screamed.

Shining white teeth spread in a reptilian grin.

"You're welcome," said the Dragon King.

Chapter Seventeen

Chastity wasn't her real name, of course. She wasn't sure if she'd ever been given a proper name. Her mother had always called her Little Red Witch. The men who had come and gone from Mother's life and bed usually called her Princess. Mostly as a joke; skinny, shy, and bruised as she'd been, she was anything but regal.

She'd grown up watching her mother make a fool of herself for the sake of love, and she'd made up her mind that she would always be given her due respect from any and all men. When yet another man left Mother, usually in a hurricane of tears and exchanged curses, she shook her head and told herself, "Any man who does that to me had better earn his keep."

When she was thirteen, she sold her virginity to a blue-eyed man with sandy brown hair and a careless smile. He paid her six gold coins for the favor, more money than Mother had seen in years. He was the one who gave her the name Chastity, and she liked the sound of it so she kept it.

Half the gold she hid, and the rest she spent on fancy clothes and perfumes that she kept in a locked box under her bed. After that, her career was made. She worked her way up from travelers to businessmen to bankers, and finally to the clean, well-kept brothel where she thought she would spend the rest of her career. But the universe had other plans for her.

She was deeply upset when she found out that Reuben had fled Lord Dark's house, but she was not surprised. The boy had always had a wild, wandering spirit. He hadn't been cut out for life as a banker. Perhaps he would join an army or become a mercenary. The idea that he would come to harm never entered her mind. He was a wizard's son. He was fated for a great destiny. The wizard himself had told her, in the heat of the night they'd spent together.

But then the dreams started.

At first she thought they were stress dreams, brought on by concern for her son. But as time went on they got darker and darker, until she was waking up two or three times a night, shaking and whimpering with fear. She dreamed of dragons, of fire, of an enormous conflagration that engulfed the whole of the Walled Kingdom. The great walls that had been built to protect them all from invaders became a prison when the land within burned with white-hot fire.

She was ordered by the brothel's madam to seek medical assistance when her lack of sleep started to affect her beauty. The madam handed her a pouch of silver and copper coins and would not hear a word of argument. Chastity rubbed her eyes, which were dark and lined from exhaustion, and obeyed silently.

But she didn't go to the doctor. Instead she went to the Dark's household, to learn what she could about her son. The Lady would have her horsewhipped if she knew what Chastity was, so she dressed in the long robes of a seer and covered her red hair with a wimple. She pretended to be a traveling witch, hoping to earn a few coppers by telling fortunes. Lady Dark was suspicious but also curious, and she let the seer in.

Chastity called herself Mag and made a great show of reading Lady Dark's palm, tea leaves, and a scattering of white stones. "You have lost someone," she intoned, trying to sound mystical and feeling foolish. "Not family, but someone close. Yes?"

"Yes." Lady Dark's tone was contemptuous. "My husband's bastard ran away a fortnight ago. No family of mine, but you could say we were related." She sniffed.

"The stars are looking at him. They see a great destiny. They are following his tracks to the… north?"

Lady Dark shrugged. "I wouldn't know. This is boring. I want to learn about my future."

Chastity would get nothing more out of this one, so she made up on the spot a glorious future with dark-eyed young men wearing brilliant smiles and little else. The Lady was sufficiently satisfied, and she paid her well before sending her on her way.

As Chastity started back toward town, a young woman ran after her. She was chubby and sullen around the eyes, and she wore the uniform of a serving girl. "I know you," she murmured, glancing over her shoulder. "You're Reuben's mother."

Chastity felt her eyes widen, but the sullen-faced girl smiled suddenly. "It's all right. She doesn't know. You look just like him, that's how I figured it out. The Lady tried to never look at him, so she wouldn't have seen."

The chubby lass had been a friend of Reuben's while he lived here, and she spoke well of the boy.

They walked into town together, sharing stories about him. Missy hated Lady Dark, and she'd enjoyed the obvious way that Chastity had fooled the woman and gotten away with it. This made her tongue loose and her mood expansive.

"I knew he had to have magical lineage, just from looking at him," Missy mused as they wandered over a bridge. Chastity paused and looked down into the muddy water, and Missy stood beside her. "He was so quiet, but so smart. He was better than me at stealing, even. Like a little robber bird. I knew his mother had to be a witch."

"His magic comes from his father's side, not mine. You taught my son to steal?"

"You should be proud of how quickly he picked it up. And of course you're a witch. You have witch's hair." Missy touched Chastity's forehead, where a lock of red hair had escaped her wimple.

Chastity jerked her head away. She was quickly tiring of this angry little woman. "My son has a great destiny in front of him. He is not meant to spend his days as a petty thief. And I am no witch."

"Not a true witch, no." Missy was suddenly serious. "But everyone in my family has the sight, and I can see the magic in you. You could probably be an herb wife, if you learned how. Reuben's aura was stronger. Probably from his father, like you said."

"I've never heard of the sight. It must be an amazing gift."

"It's a curse." Missy sighed and leaned over the rickety railing. Something creaked, and Chastity's heart jumped. "I can see into people's souls, see all the bad feelings inside of them. Lady Dark hates everyone. It's torture to work for her. I try to embarrass her and make her cry to distract her from hating everyone. I used to try to make her laugh, but she likes to hate too much. It makes her feel strong."

"Why don't you leave? Work for someone else."

"I'm going to leave. I'm going to leave right now. If you see Reuben again, give him my love."

The railing creaked again, and something snapped. Missy smiled at Chastity, gave a little hop, and then she was gone, into the swirling, murky water.

Chastity never went back to the brothel. She went to the Walled City's book shop instead, and she spent almost every penny she had on books about witches and herb wives.

She hoped to one day catch up to Reuben on his travels, but she never did. Instead she set up shop in a secluded little village, far away from cities and whorehouses. Every stream and river ran crystal clear, with no mysteries within.

****

Helene sat bolt upright in bed. On the floor nearby, Roger stirred. "What is it?" he mumbled.

"I don't know." Helene looked around the dark room. Of course there was nothing to see. The chapter had just ended; all was still in the universe of the Walled Kingdom.

After dodging the harpy scouts, they had finally delivered Ember to the herb witch Mag. They were supposed to move on after this, hopefully drawing the attention of the Dragon King away from the child. Roger had the idea of stealing or buying a slave child to take along as bait, but Helene wasn't sure. If something happened to the decoy baby, she'd never forgive herself. Or Roger.

With or without bait, they should have left yesterday. But something kept them here in the witch's hut. (Roger could call her what he liked; to Helene that woman would always be Mag the Witch.) No spell or trance held them, but the twin demons of uncertainty and love. Helene didn't want to leave the baby with a strange woman she'd never met: a woman whose hut smelled of strange smoke and male company. Mag claimed that the men coming and going from her hut were clients paying for potions and poultices, but Helene caught the sly looks between them and surmised that in addition to magic, Mag provided other types of essential services.

That was nothing to Helene; any woman was free to make money however she saw fit. But she worried about the men who came and went. Could a double agent be among them, seeking out Mag as a way to gain access to Ember?

Her second reason for lingering was simpler and more primal. After so many weeks of caring for the child she didn't want to leave her. Feeding and protecting the little one had awakened a maternal feeling in her breast that made her feel lonely and empty when she thought about moving on.

Roger hadn't offered an opinion either way. He was the same as he'd always been: strong, loyal, and almost utterly silent.

Until the chapter ended or the scene shifted; only then was he free to speak his mind.

"What's she thinking, keeping us here?" he grumbled one night after retiring and 'falling into an uneasy sleep.' "This is getting boring."

"She's building up tension," Helene responded. She opened a window and stuck her head outside. It was eerie to see the perfect stillness of a scene change; the trees still bent in the night wind, but there was no wind. "There's either going to be a tremendous revelation about Mag, or something big is going to attack the village and kill everyone. Maybe both."

"How do you know this?"

"I read *Imprisonment of Hope* eight times. I know her style."

Now Helene sat on the scratchy straw bed and peered around the room. It was dark and still as ever. The stars outside shone clear as glass with nary a twinkle. Helene stomped her foot on the earthen floor, and it made the same almost-silent scuff. Even sound was muted during chapter breaks; the only clear sounds were Helene and Roger's voices.

All was as it had been, but something had startled her out of her drowse. Nothing from this world, inside the Book. She knew the feeling of a chapter starting again; the air would freshen and her mind would no longer be entirely her own. It was unnerving to be at the mercy of the narrative, but it was better than dying of dragon dust.

Had something happened to Diana? What would that mean to them, if she was unable to finish the book? Would they be trapped here in the dark forever, stuck between chapters? What a horrible thought. Surely someone would discover the manuscript and finish the story. But it wouldn't be as good. Ghostwritten books never were.

Helene didn't have a bad feeling about Diana, though. She didn't really have a bad feeling at all, just an uneasy one. Like something could happen, but hadn't yet. Or had happened, but it hadn't gone completely wrong yet. She shook her head. Now she was confused.

"Is everything all right?" Roger asked.

Helene spoke without thinking. "There's something wrong with the shop." Then her hand flew to her mouth. She didn't know where the words had come from, but she knew that they were true.

Roger sat up quickly. The shop was his only home. "What's wrong? The boogeyman?"

"Yes. No. He's still in his book. I think. But something is leaking out. Something got out, but not him. Something worse. What could be worse?"

"We need to get back there. You're the only one who knows how to take care of the shop."

"Diana's still there. She's a witch."

"Yes but she doesn't know the shop like you do. Remember what happened to Francine?"

Helene remembered. But there was nothing she could do while she was trapped in Diana Druid's narrative. So she sat in the silent, unnatural darkness and her unease grew and grew.

****

Reuben slept on the scrubby couch in the living room of Helene's apartment. He slept because he'd been drinking for hours, and he'd been drinking because he felt completely out of place and useless. It was as bad as the years he had spent in the home of the banker, Mr. Dark. Worse, because his youth and his destiny were both behind him. He knew who his father was, and he was no great wizard. His father was a scheming dragon who had fled the harsh northern mountains and sought dominion over the soft, civilized humans trapped behind their precious walls. Reuben was no chosen one. Just a whore's bastard, and his great miraculous destiny was to be a cat's paw and scapegoat. He deserved every scrap of his misery and more, after the way he'd betrayed the people of the Walled Kingdom. He was a fool.

He woke blearily and reached for the bottle on the floor next to the couch. It was empty, but he shook it anyway, as though he could wish more tequila into existence. He wanted to drink himself to death, but he wasn't sure it was possible. Over the years he had discovered that he was very hard to kill.

Francine was gone, stolen away into the other realm of that dark spirit haunting the book shop. Diana had promised to find a way to bring him back, but Reuben knew that his beloved was not a top priority. She never had been. Diana had hated Francine from the moment of her creation, and she had forgotten about her when she'd rewritten *Imprisonment of Hope*. Even now she didn't recognize the name, or maybe she thought it a coincidence that Reuben's love had the same name of an erased bit character.

Diana's only objective was to kill the Dragon King. The last book was here, and victory was finally within her grasp. She might try to reunite Reuben with Francine if it fit the narrative, but if it did not then she would never give it another thought.

Nothing was more important than the story Diana was telling to herself.

All of this rolled around in the front of Reuben's mind, effectively blocking out the nagging, slithering voice at the back of his brain. The voice that was the real reason he was drunk. The voice of his father. It spoke every time he closed his eyes, and it told him terrible, hateful things. It was that voice that had driven him to the rage that had triggered his attack on Helene. He could still feel the gritty dragon dust between his fingers.

The voice knew about Diana's new book. It knew what was in it, because Reuben knew. And it wanted him to do one last thing, perform one last task as the son of the Dragon King.

And in spite of everything, Reuben wanted to do it. He wanted to make his father proud of him. And he knew that was ridiculous. His father saw him as nothing but another weak human, albeit one with pointed teeth. The Dragon King would taunt and torment him into doing his bidding, then he would laugh at Reuben's guilt. As he had done over and over again.

But still, he wanted to do it. He wanted to burn the book.

And so he drank.

His father's voice still called to him, urgently. Hints of mockery that faded as the King's voice echoed louder and louder in Reuben's tequila-sodden brain. He reached for the bottle again, knocking it over. But shit, it was empty anyway. Maybe Brach would buy him another bottle, if he asked nicely. Brach seemed to like him, even if Diana didn't.

"Reuben, wake up."

"I'm not doing it, Father," Reuben said without looking around. He knew he would see nobody. It was all in his head, so to speak.

The Dragon King's voice was low and menacing. "Oh, I think you will. If you value your precious love."

Against his own common sense, Reuben looked around the empty room. "What are you talking about?"

He blinked slowly, and in the moment that his eyes were closed he saw Francine, pinned and helpless in the black claws of his father. "No!" Reuben shouted. His eyes flew open, and the image vanished.

"I have her. She slipped out of the Book while the boogeyman was occupied, and now she is mine. Borders are breaking down, and the rules are changing. If you do what I ask, it will all go up in flames. And then I can start over, with you at my side."

With the wild magic that bubbled up under the shop. That ley line crossing was what the scaly bastard really wanted. It was frightening to imagine what he could do with that kind of power at his disposal. Reuben had once hoped that he could use that power to bring Francine back to life, but now the bastard had Francine. Would he keep his old promise if Reuben did what he wanted?

He honestly didn't know. The Dragon King could keep a promise if it suited him. Was there any incentive to keep this one?

"If I do this, will you let her go?" he asked. His voice trembled. "And let me use some of the power of the shop to bring her back? You can do that, right?"

"Of course. Why would I not? I gave her to you, didn't I?"

Indeed he had. The night of All Hallow's Eve, Reuben had snuck into a costume party in this building, and the Dragon King had guided him through a ritual that would summon her as a character. There had been a copy of *Imprisonment of Hope* on one of the book shelves, and Reuben had made it part of the ritual. Then, after Francine had appeared in his arms, so beautiful and loving, they had performed a second rite that should have brought the Dragon King through from the book-world of the Walled Kingdom. That ritual had gone less successfully, and Reuben's father never let him forget that he had given his son a gift and had gotten nothing in return.

But she had been a gift with a twist, a lovely piece of bait with a very carefully hidden hook. A hook so concealed that even Francine had no idea it was there. She still thought she was a normal mortal woman who had died the night of that apocalyptic party.

She didn't remember that she'd actually died many years before. In another time, and in another world. Diana had forgotten, and so had she.

"Will you do it?" the King's voice cut deeply into his head. The hangover was setting in.

A heavy ball of misgiving settled into Reuben's gut, and not even the most profuse bout of vomiting would dislodge it. "I'll do it," he whispered.

"Swear to me on your mother's name."

Vellichor

"I swear to you on Chastity's name, may she outlive you by a thousand years."

The Dragon King chuckled. "Your mother is dead, as you well know. As curses go, you could have done better."

Reuben lay back down and covered his face with a cushion. He wasn't sure if his father could see him or not, but just to be sure he didn't not want to expose his expression of relief.

The King didn't know as much as he thought he did.

****

Diana's body jerked, and she slammed both hands across the keyboard. The letters skittered across the paper, marring her story with gibberish. She spat a curse and slapped the desk beside the machine. What the hell just happened?

"Brach!" she said. "Brach, are you all right?"

She had no reason to think that he wasn't; he'd been minding the shop all morning without event. There hadn't been a whiff of anything weird, aside from the random characters hanging around the desk, asking where Helene was and when she'd be back. The young hippie girl, Jazzy, seemed particularly concerned. She asked about Helene's welfare so often she sounded more like a hovering mother than a casual acquaintance.

Brach appeared in the doorway with a puzzled expression. "Sure. Why wouldn't I be?"

"Where's Reuben?"

"Upstairs, passed out drunk. He hasn't moved from the couch since we opened, except to get up and piss out some tequila. It's a wonder you can't smell it down here."

"Why is he drinking so much?"

"Don't know, and don't really care. As long as he stays quiet and in one place, he can drink 'til the cows come home."

Everything seemed all right, but Diana didn't like it. She was a creature of instinct, used to following her gut without question. Often it led her into trouble, like when she'd written *Imprisonment of Hope* in the first place. But when she got a bad feeling for no apparent reason, she knew she would do well to heed that feeling.

That weird, convulsive twitch on the keyboard had been the start. She'd been typing along, finally moving Helene and Roger into a position to find out the true nature of the red-headed witch they'd brought the baby to, and suddenly her whole body had seized up in an all-over spasm. It was like—she had no idea what it was like. Strychnine poisoning, maybe, though she had never experienced it firsthand.

Her heart was still galloping like a runaway pony. She hoped she wasn't having a stroke. Her blood pressure had been perfectly healthy at her last doctor visit, but how long ago had that been? She'd been chasing a monster for thirty years; she wasn't getting any younger.

And if she didn't finish the job here and now, it would never get done. She still had no faith in her ability to bring Helene back, so forward was the only way to go. She had to finish the book.

"Is it getting dark in here?" Brach asked.

It was, and Diana paused in her musings to look around the cluttered office. It was well-lit by fluorescent lights overhead as well as a charming antique lamp on the desk next to the computer. There was no natural light at all, and no indication of a power interruption that could make the light seem dimmer. But dimmer it was. As though a veil had been drawn across the light.

"Are there any customers?" she whispered.

"No," Brach whispered back. "Why are we whispering?"

"Something is here. Go close the shop. And get a handful of those silver slugs from under the register."

Brach obeyed. Diana sat in the silent office and stared at the half-filled page in the typewriter. It had been a bit of dialogue between Helene and Mag. What did it feel like to Helene right now, being stuck in midsentence? Was she aware of Diana's progress, or was it as though she was unconscious? Diana would never know.

From somewhere at the front of the shop, Brach screamed.

Diana never hesitated. She grabbed the box of salt from the shelf under Helene's computer desk and ran for the front of the shop. Just then another convulsion struck. Her body seized up, and she stiffened and fell to the floor. The box of salt landed on its side, spilling white granules across the patterned carpet. A bolt of pain shot through her right arm; she'd landed on it hard.

Diana lay still for a moment, getting her bearings. Then, very slowly, she lifted her head and looked for Brach.

She couldn't see him at first, because there was something black rippling across the floor near her face. She rolled over and pulled herself into a sitting position. Another manifestation, no doubt; maybe something out of Jules Verne. All those waving tentacles.

But then Brach screamed again, and Diana saw what held him. And she screamed too.

It was impossible. A weird creature of impossible angles and curves that hurt her mind. This thing was more than alien; it was from a place that had none of the same mathematical or physical laws that Diana knew. It hurt her mind to look at it, but that was not why she screamed.

She screamed, and screamed again, because it held Brach in its tentacles. Squeezing his body, his face swelling and turning purple.

Chapter Eighteen

It wasn't a manifestation. Diana knew that right away. Book characters lacked the power to harm a human body like this. Even the boogeyman could not actually seize and strangle a physical human body. His powers were largely those of the mind.

Diana pushed her fear and revulsion aside and held up her hands, palms out. "By the power of the light, begone from this place!" she said. Before the words had left her mouth she knew it wouldn't work. There was no sense of light, no strength of purpose. The beings of light that protected this place had fled, along with most of Diana's wits.

It was just wrong. It hurt her mind. It wasn't just a seething mass of black, slimy tentacles creeping out of the carpeted floor. It was something else. Something from Outside.

A ginger-haired figure appeared next to her. "Reuben," Diana said, and she could say no more. Her mind. It hurt her mind, and she couldn't look away.

Reuben said nothing at all. He opened a small black pouch and poured its contents into his hand. It was black powder that glittered like stars. Diana closed her eyes and turned away as he threw the fistful of dragon dust at the many-tentacled horror.

What would it do to Brach if it touched him? Too late to worry about that now. Surely anything would be better than being slowly strangled to death by that horrible thing from Outside.

As the dragon dust landed, the thing's roiling motion ceased. It didn't shrivel or collapse; it only slowed. Brach was still caught in its grip, but his wild, frantic motions also slowed, and his eyes went blank and still.

"Come on," Reuben said. "Let's get him out of there. It's not going to last long."

Diana followed him as he clambered over the tentacles toward the trapped man. Now that she was among them, they didn't seem quite so horrible. Weird and gross, yes, but they were just tentacles. Like any squid or octopus might have.

Until she caught a glimpse of the underside of one of them. Instead of suckers, it was covered with tiny screaming faces. Diana shivered and looked away.

Reuben was carefully prying a tentacle as big around as his fist off Brach's neck. "Get his legs," he grunted. "And hurry. It's trying to react."

Diana glanced down. She stood on a thick, ropy tentacle the size of a tree branch, and as she watched it seemed to flex like a muscle. The thing wasn't completely paralyzed. It was just very, very slow.

She scrambled the rest of the way to Brach and yanked the tentacles off his legs. They came away with a series of pops and rips, like tearing Velcro. The faces on the tentacle were biting Brach's legs, and as Diana tore them away they took bits of thread and fabric with them. Where Reuben had succeeded in pulling the tentacle off his neck, Diana saw a neat pattern of bloody pinpricks.

Vellichor

She shuddered and pulled harder. At last Brach was mostly free, though his face remained still, and his face was still bright red with a flush of purple.

Together she and Reuben hauled his stiff body out of the mass of tentacles and into the relative safety of the back office. Brach still didn't move.

"It's the dragon dust." Reuben was sweaty and out of breath. Diana didn't feel so hot herself. Her heart was pounding, and her hands felt ice-cold and sweaty. That convulsion that had struck her just before the tentacle horror had attacked them still left her feeling shaken and off balance.

When had she last eaten? Shit. That was what she both loved and hated about writing. It took her away from the world, but often at the expense of her health.

Reuben was still talking, and she tried to focus on his words. "I was able to charge the dust with time, so we could get in there and get him out. But he got a hit of it too, and it will take a while to wear off."

"You charged it with time?" Diana blinked.

"Dragons can slow time in small doses, to help them travel faster and strike quicker. Since I'm half dragon, I can empower the dust to do dragon things."

Oh yes, Diana remembered the time bubble device. A one-time cheat she'd used to get the Dragon King to a certain battle in time to turn the tide. She regretted that deus ex machina, since she'd had no further use for it beyond that scene, but apparently her lazy writing had paid off for once.

They looked back at the stiff, slow-moving creature. Diana was again reminded that this was no manifestation; it was a real, actual creature that had somehow appeared in the shop. She had no idea how to get rid of it. And the danger wasn't over; if Brach would soon recover from the effects of the dust, so would it.

"We need Helene back," Diana said. "The boogeyman said that the wild magic is getting out of control. This must be what he meant. They aren't just projections of stories anymore. They're becoming real."

"Like me," Reuben said softly. Diana glanced at him, but his face was distant and neutral.

She didn't know what the hell to do. She hadn't felt this helpless since she'd been paroled. Always she'd been able to come up with an idea, have a plan for the next step. Even if she didn't know the whole way up the ladder, she always knew what the next rung or two looked like, and that was usually enough. If something went wrong, then she'd scrap that idea and start on the next one. It was how she'd lived her entire life, and it had rarely steered her wrong.

But now she couldn't steer at all. She was lost at sea, and a storm was churning her entire world into chaos and death. This monster had no doubt escaped the boogeyman's collection of short stories. It looked like an homage to Cthuhlu and Lovecraft. What was next?

Imprisonment of Hope still sat on the front desk, next to the register. No one had dared touch it since Diana had tried to burn it, and even the customers seemed to avoid it.

Vellichor

If that horrendous thing could escape from its book, really escape and not just manifest a projection, would the Dragon King be next?

"I have an idea," Reuben said. "Can I see your book again?"

"The new one?" Diana knew what book he meant, but she had misgivings about letting him touch it again. There was something about his eyes she didn't like. They were too blue, too bright in the dim light of the office. "What do you want with it?"

"If that thing came through—really came through—maybe Helene can too."

"But she'll still be poisoned by the dragon dust."

"If I act quickly enough, I can neutralize it. That's why I need to touch the book."

Diana looked into his odd blue eyes. Flecks of gold seemed to drift in his azure irises, another detail she'd forgotten she'd written. He was so much more complicated than she remembered.

On the floor at her feet, Brach's arms shifted a bit, and the flush in his face faded as he took a breath. He was slowly coming out of the time bubble, which meant that there wasn't much time left. The tentacled horror would also recover. And what if it had friends, waiting in the Book behind it?

"All right. Help me get him further away from this door." Diana hoped she wasn't making a mistake.

Reuben carried Brach's shoulders and dragged him further back. Diana held his legs, and she could feel the stiffened flesh begin to soften beneath her fingers. Time was running out.

"It's right there," she said, pointing at the stack of pages. Hand typed, with no backup copy. It was the most precious thing in the world to her, and she was about to let the heir of the Dragon King touch it.

"Trust me," Reuben said. "I know what I'm doing. Everything will go back to normal after this." He reached into his pocket and took out a pinch of dragon dust.

He glanced back at her one last time, and Diana saw the gold in his eyes, brighter than ever. As she watched, the gold flecks swarmed and overtook the blue. The Dragon King looked out of Reuben Dark's eyes.

"No!" She leaped at him, but she tripped over Brach's prone body and went sprawling. Her body was still shaking and confused after those two odd seizures earlier. Her knee caught the edge of a metal filing cabinet, and she screamed a curse. White-hot agony bolted up her leg, and she felt like she might piss herself.

As though time had slowed for all of them, Diana looked up to see Reuben sprinkle dragon dust over the stack of newborn infant pages. The black dust sparkled like gold dust as it fell.

And the pages burst into flame.

****

Christopher danced from foot to foot. He felt off-kilter and out of place, as though the ground beneath his feet was shifting. Francine had disappeared silently into the white space between the words, and there was no sign of what had become of her.

"Francine?" he called, feeling useless and stupid. "Are you okay?"

202

Vellichor

No answer, of course. Maybe she'd made it back to the shop, to that One True Love of hers. Maybe he should have told her the truth about him, and about her. But she probably wouldn't have believed him. Anything the boogeyman said would be taken as a lie, and Christopher had no other evidence. Just the boogeyman's amused comments, and his own sickly gut telling him that every word was true.

"Yo, asshole," he said. There was no need to shout. The boogeyman was never far away, since space didn't matter here.

A cold, skeletal presence manifested near his right shoulder. "Your companion has abandoned us," the boogeyman observed.

"Is she all right? Did she make it back to the shop?"

"Yes. And no. The Dragon King won't harm her while he can use her to manipulate his son, but she didn't win her freedom."

"You were telling the truth, weren't you? Francine isn't what she thinks she is. That's why the exorcism didn't work."

"Let this be a lesson to all would-be writers and storytellers. Don't be lazy, and never forget a character. You never know where they'll end up."

"But she did die in the fire."

"To the extent that a fictional character can die. She originally died in the Walled Kingdom, of course, but even then Diana was playing around with reality, and the Dragon King was able to sneak her through, using Reuben of course. Her second death, at the party, was the perfect opportunity for the Dragon King to re-shape her memories and make her believe what he wanted her to. It was a way to get another pair of eyes in the real world, and a hook in Reuben that transcended worlds."

"What's he doing with her now?"

"I have no idea. Right now she's the least of our worries. There's a fire in the shop, and the whole place is about to go up like yesterday's kindling."

"What?" Christopher's heart seemed to burst with fear. "How? What can we do? Why aren't you doing something?"

"Young man, I can't do anything. I'm not real, and everyone knows it. Nobody believes in me anymore, so all I can do is jump out and say boo. Shall I try to frighten the fire away?"

"Oh fuck you." This was no time for dry wit. "But they do believe in me, right? Can you send me back?"

The boogeyman's shroud ripped in the semblance of a shrug. "I can try. But with Helene gone from the real world, I can't promise you anything. And the Dragon King's still just outside my borders."

"Please try. I have to do something."

"Very well. Try to save my Book, if you do nothing else."

****

Diana squatted and tried to lift Brach into her arms. But he was so stiff, so heavy, and the dragon dust made her muscles feel stiff and slow. Something in her lower back popped audibly, and she shouted a curse. This wasn't going to work.

Then someone was beside her, lifting Brach's other arm, and together they shoved the old man's time-stiffened body at the burning pages. Diana hoped that the residual dragon dust would slow the burn so that she could save most of the book. Brach toppled slowly toward the typewriter, shedding black sprinkles as he fell. Belatedly Diana realized that Brach could be horribly burned, and she hoped that the slowing of time would also slow the damage to Brach's thin old skin.

Brach toppled, and as he fell Diana saw one hand twitch and reach out. The effect of the dust was wearing off.

His hand glanced off the edge of the desk, and his body toppled to the floor. Diana had missed, and the book continued to burn.

She glanced at her companion and was not surprised at all to see Christopher. "He let you go?"

"I don't think he can hold me anymore," Christopher said. He stared at Reuben with complete loathing. "The barriers all over the shop are breaking down. You can bring Helene back."

Diana shook her head. "She's in there," she whispered. She pointed at the flames, which were spreading to the rest of the desk. "I can't bring her back out of there."

"Yes you can. And you have to. Because—"

The lights went out. The office was dark, lit only by the crackling glow of the spreading fire.

"Diana?" Brach's voice was bleary. "What happened? My head is killing me."

"It's not as bad as you think," Christopher whispered. "You can do this. Helene is the anchor, the one holding the wild magic in place. The little creatures were never attracted to the salt or the cinnamon. It was always her. Just like her aunt before her. But now the shop is flooding with wild magic, and none of us will survive the night if you don't bring her back."

Diana looked around. In the doorway of the office, a dozen—no, dozens—of faces peered at her. Mostly human, all different ages and races, some in modern garb and others in tattered rags. Close to the floor a warren's worth of rabbits and two anthropomorphic bears stared at her with wide black eyes.

"She's not just in the book," Christopher hissed. "She never was. She's in there." And he thumped her on the head with a sharp knuckle. It didn't hurt. In fact, she barely felt it.

"Now bring her back!"

Chapter Nineteen

Bring her back. Diana closed her eyes and took a breath. Never mind the gathering darkness, the tentacled thing that was probably waking up this very second, never mind Brach, still sprawled on the floor and trying desperately to sit up. Never mind Reuben, who was staring at the burning desk as though awaiting further instruction. Perhaps he was. How strong was the Dragon King's hold on him? How stupid was Diana for not killing him ages ago?

No, this was not the time for that. No self-hatred, no sackcloth and ashes allowed here. Later she could look back on this and scream at herself for all the mistakes she'd made. Now was not the time.

As Diana took another breath and tried to still her scrambling mind, a young woman with black hair and a paisley smock appeared at her side. "Can I help?" she asked. Her voice was low and a little faint.

Diana glanced at her. It was Jazzy again, the little-hippie-that-could from Memoirs. Helene had taken hours to decide if that book should go in Literary Fiction instead, since she'd read that most of the story was fabricated. But she'd decided on Memoirs after all, after Diana had pointed out that no writer worth his or her royalty ever told the full truth about themselves.

"Jazz," Diana said.

The young woman nodded. "I want to help you get Helene back. He—we're all really worried." She glanced back at the office doorway, where faces and bodies still crowded in spite of the rising temperature.

"Helene is dead," Reuben said clearly. "Your sequel is gone. You can't stop him now." His eyes glittered gold in the firelight.

Diana couldn't believe that. She had to believe that Christopher was right, that there was a way to save the shop and their own lives too. Surely Christopher would know. He belonged to Helene.

"Diana," he said urgently. "Please."

Yes, okay, she knew what she had to do. But she didn't know how to start! How could she even reach Helene from here, let alone bring her back?

Reuben stood in front of the fire, which had spread to a stack of mail next to the typewriter. And Diana thought she knew what to do.

When in doubt, close your eyes and jump, she thought.

She grabbed Jazz by the hand, jumped over Brach's still-prone body, and launched herself at Reuben. He ducked instinctively, and she easily knocked him aside as she and Jazzy fell face-first into the fire.

There was a flash of burning heat that scorched Diana's face, and she smelled burning hair. Shit! It hadn't worked, and now she was on fire. This was a hell of a way to die.

But the heat faded, and Diana felt cool air on her face. She squeezed Jazzy's hand, and the girl squeezed back. They were still alive then, and they didn't seem to be burning to death. One of Jazzy's thick braids slapped her in the face and stung like a whip crack.

Vellichor

Diana dared to open her eyes, hoping like hell that the fire was not near her face. She looked around, and dimly she could see Jazzy's round face. There was a flicker of light from somewhere that came and went like a slow strobe. Diana looked up and down, but she could not find a source for the light flickers.

This wasn't the Walled Kingdom or any place like it. "Where are we?" she asked, as though Jazzy would have any idea.

But the hippie surprised her. "We're in the darkness between pages. You need to find the story that you want. I never read it, so I don't know what it looks like."

Diana looked all around. In the dancing flickers she saw vague black shapes that moved and danced just out of sight. Some were wide and blocky, resembling shelves. Then they flickered and changed, and Diana saw tunnels and roads that bent in odd angles. Then the darkness changed again, and Diana had to close her eyes. It was making her brain hurt.

"I don't know how to do this," she confessed.

Jazzy squeezed her hand. "Just picture the world inside the book. Smell the air, feel the soil. Don't pretend we're there: be there."

The Walled Kingdom was a beautiful place, full of wonders. And dragons, she thought, but she pushed that image away. Instead she thought about the green grass, the swaying trees, the little bird people that lived in the weeping willow and made it dance whenever it rained. She thought about Unseen Valley, and the Lost Village where the last chosen warrior had taken refuge. Helene and Roger were still there, unsure of where to go next. That was where her story had ended.

And it had been burned to smithereens by that bastard Reuben. She fancied she could still smell the acrid smoke of burning pages.

"Stop it," Jazz hissed. "Everything you imagine can turn real here. It's the darkness between pages, and it's full of wild magic."

Green grass, green grass and bird people. Clever Valley, within it the Lost Village. It had probably rained recently, since it always rained, so no fire was possible.

"I think we're here," Jazzy whispered.

Diana opened her eyes. She felt—ordinary. She looked up, and there was the brilliant blue sky with its characteristic tinge of purple. The sun was low in the sky, more red than yellow. The grass below her feet was thick and springy, and she smelled the sweet flowers in the puff of breeze that tickled her nose and played with her hair.

She knew this place. She knew every inch, every scent, every bird and beast that lived here. This was her world, the Walled Kingdom.

But what surprised her most was how unsurprised she felt. Jazzy stared around with her mouth ajar, taking in the magic and the newness. A sparkling butterfly danced past, its wings glinting like foil in the evening sun. Jazzy jumped, and she laughed aloud. Diana smiled too, and she wished she could experience everything new and strange like Jazzy. But she couldn't. She had been here too many times in her dreams. Now, all she felt was relief that they'd made it after all, and urgency to find Helene and get her out.

Vellichor

"How do I find Helene?" she asked herself aloud.

But Jazz answered. "Aren't you God here? You can find anyone."

Of course. Diana looked around at the rolling green mountains, and she pointed in a random direction. "The Unseen Valley is just out of sight that way," she said.

"Then let's go." And off they went.

****

Reuben felt a rush of triumph as the fire danced and spread across the pages of the book. His spell had come off perfectly; it looked exactly as though he'd set the book on fire, like he'd promised the Dragon King. It was even real fire. One had to look very, very closely to see that the book was not actually burning. Finally something was going right in his life.

Since he was a boy he'd worked for his father: spreading dissension, killing children of certain noble bloodlines, and in this world he'd conducted rituals at every ley line crossing he could find to try to summon him to this world. The last one, thirty years ago, had almost worked. Father had managed to push through a very small opening, but something on this side had shoved him back. He'd blasted the place with dragon fire, but the passageway had closed.

Now Reuben knew why it hadn't worked. Even before the book shop had existed the local spirits had protected this sacred place. He should have taken the hint that he was working for the wrong side. He'd tried to convince himself that being with his father, helping and protecting the one who had given him life, was the only important aspect of his existence. Certainly his mother had drilled it into him often enough that his low heritage was nothing to savor. Only his paternity mattered, and only his father's opinion mattered to him. He had been foolish, but now at last he hoped that he had made up for some of it.

Brach was still on the floor of the office, but he was finally moving freely, climbing to his feet. "Reuben," he gasped. "I trusted you. I thought you were all right."

Reuben didn't dare speak out loud. He wasn't sure how much the Dragon King could hear. "You should have read the book," he said. He edged away, toward the office door. It was getting hot in here.

Brach was bent over like an old, old man. He too staggered away from the spreading flames. A few sparks popped and drifted to the cheap plastic carpeting. "Trusted you," he repeated. His blue eyes were rimmed with red.

Brach charged at Reuben, head down like a bull. Reuben reacted without thinking. He braced himself and held his hands apart as though about to catch a ball. Brach slammed into Reuben's slender body—and stopped dead. Reuben shoved him backward. "You should have trusted your girlfriend, not me," he said.

The fire had spread to some papers on the floor, and Brach fell into them. Dragon fire was attracted to living flesh, and it swarmed over him eagerly. Brach's screams were mercifully brief. Perhaps he'd already been dying of a heart attack or stroke, or perhaps the dragon fire had been starving because of the diet Reuben's spell had put it on. It didn't matter. Reuben had done what the Dragon King asked, and now he would be reunited with his lovely Francine.

"I'm ready, Father," he said aloud.

"Ready for what?" the Dragon King murmured in his ear.

Reuben turned his head, but the dragon wasn't there. Not yet, maybe not ever now. "I burned the book, and I killed the writer's lover. I want Francine back now, please. Where is she?"

"I have no idea. And I don't care. You failed me, you little bastard."

"Failed you? But I did what you asked!"

"I told you to stop the witch writer, but she's here. She's in the Walled Kingdom. Bending space to her whim and taking back her precious heroes. You failed me, son. I'm done with you."

"You never told me to stop Diana. You told me to burn the books. I did. Where's Francine?"

"What I said is that I'm done with you. Find the girl yourself. If you survive long enough."

And Reuben was completely alone. His head was empty of all thoughts but his own, and he was surrounded by spreading flames. They seemed to sense his presence, and they crept across the floor in his direction.

Reuben dashed for the door, singeing his clothes in the process. He couldn't die in fire; it was one of the advantages of being dragon spawn. But it was still unpleasant, and his skin could be horribly scorched. He hoped that he had escaped serious injury as he opened the door and slipped through to the larger shop.

The air was comparatively cool and fresh out here, and Reuben took a moment to catch his breath. He had gotten away with his deception; that was most important. If the Dragon King had detected Reuben's betrayal, he would have gone mad with rage and tried to kill him. But Reuben didn't understand what he'd meant when he said that he didn't know where Francine was. If the King was toying with him and didn't want to give Francine back, he would have come out and said so. If he intended to extort further favors or magic, he would have said that too. So he must have been telling the truth. But how could he not know where Francine was? There was no way a little slip like her could have escaped.

All such thoughts were driven out of his mind in a heartbeat, when he looked up into the waving mass of black tentacles that now filled the shop from floor to ceiling.

The Thing stank of cesspools and the bottom of the sea. Dead fish and sludge. The aroma made him cough. He reached into his pocket, but it came up empty. He was out of dragon dust.

I should have just burned everything to the ground from the start, he thought bitterly. Father's book, too. It would have gotten everything over quicker. This is hell, and I'm trapped in it.

"Hello there," said a young man standing next to him.

Reuben stared. The skinny fellow seemed unafraid of the writhing tentacles; one slapped the wood-paneled wall behind him, tearing off a chunk. The stranger didn't even flinch.

"Who are you?" Reuben asked. Another manifestation, no doubt. They were everywhere, and they never knew how to mind their own business.

"Just a figment of your imagination. Or maybe you're a figment of mine. I forget which. Are you alive?" The young man looked around as he spoke, as though he was looking for something. Or someone.

"Yes." That was true enough. For thirty years Reuben had lived and breathed in this world, eaten and drank and evacuated his bowels (something he'd never done in his life while living in the Walled Kingdom.) His origins were suspect, but he was as alive as a man could be.

"What do you think, boss?" the stranger asked over his shoulder. "Is this close enough? Will he do?"

"Close enough for horse shoes. He'll do perfectly."

Something cold and hard wrapped around his throat. Reuben gasped and clutched at it with both hands, but it was not choking him. A cold circlet of bones was wrapped around his neck and pulled him firmly, implacably, toward the writhing mass of tentacles.

Reuben thrashed and kicked, and one of his feet caught a nearby tentacle. Instantly it wrapped around his legs and squeezed. Reuben screamed. He couldn't remember the last time he'd felt pain.

The circlet of bone vanished, but it was replaced by the slimy, fleshy arm of the Thing. Reuben stopped screaming as his air was cut off.

As he descended into the final darkness, he wondered if Francine would be waiting for him.

****

Christopher looked away as the Tentacled Horror (its actual name, according to the short story from which it had sprung) made a rapid end of the Dragon King's misbegotten son. The fucker deserved it, but that didn't mean Christopher wanted to stand around and watch justice being served. The boogeyman seemed to watch avidly, though it was hard to tell what that bony, shrouded face was looking at.

"Did the sacrifice work?" he asked. "Can you banish it now?"

"Yes. But I don't know how much good it will do. The next time someone crosses the veil it will get loose again. It or something like it."

Christopher was familiar with most of the dark things lurking between the pages of the boogeyman's book, and he shivered. "Diana and Jazzy went in after Helene. Will everything go back to normal once they bring her back?"

The boogeyman's shroud ripped, his version of a shrug. "Does anything ever go back to normal after it's been shattered?"

"I wouldn't know." Christopher watched as the boogeyman's shroud rose and expanded, swirling around the tentacles and slowly drawing them back toward Sci Fi/Fantasy/Horror. The lights overhead came on again, and Christopher sighed. Maybe nothing could really go back to normal, but he'd settle for a little peace.

As the last crawling arm slid back into the book, the boogeyman reappeared and took Christopher by the arm. "Time to go," he said around his eternal, skeletal grin.

216

Vellichor

Damn it. "I don't want to go," he said. He felt like a sulking toddler.

"It's never been a habit of mine to care what you want. Let's go, before something else gets loose."

"Why can't you just let me stay in the shop?" he asked. The familiar darkness of the place between books enveloped them, and he squinted as the bright whiteness of the Book returned.

"Because you don't belong to me. You belong to Helene. She's the only one who can free you."

Christopher cocked his head. "Say that again?"

"You're Helene's creation. She's the only one who can control your destiny."

Christopher felt his heart jump with surprise, but it was a familiar sort of jump. As though he'd known this before but forgotten. Christopher didn't always remember that he wasn't exactly, specifically, technically real. Probably because Helene wasn't always sure herself.

Chapter Twenty

Roger got up and strolled out of the cottage as casually as he could. He felt like a kite on the wind, carried along by the wind on a long leash. He felt completely out of control of his own life, at the mercy of these well-meaning but overbearing females. All he could do with his own body right now was go for a walk. So that was what he did.

The cool air filled his lungs, and he tried to relax and enjoy the gentle weather of the early evening. After all, what was his life anyway? As far back as he could remember, he'd been an outdated hero trapped in a stack of books. Kill the monster, rescue the girl, save the day, lather, rinse, repeat. Each story had been the same plot with different monsters. Had he been any freer then?

There was a time when he'd been truly free, his own creature. He only remembered it in his dreams, but sometimes he awoke with a strange sadness and a feeling of something bright that was forever lost. Like a fish in the ocean, he thought—something floating free, unaware and uncaring. But the fish had been lured in by lovely bait: stories, tales, things that had never existed yet somehow created their own worlds and their own reality. The Roger-fish had been drawn into the stories and trapped there by the books. He'd been given a name. And he hadn't been the only one; other "fish" from other oceans had been similarly lured. Bright beings with wisdom and memories that extended beyond the human imagination. Most of the people living in the books at Enchanted Ink had no recollection that they'd ever been anything else. That was probably a kindness.

There had been dark things in those other worlds, too, Roger remembered. He remembered fleeing some, doing battle with others. But what he remembered most of all was the complete unstructured freedom of the place. No plot, no story, no character development. Just sheer perfect imagination.

Maybe he remembered because the books he'd come to live in were so close to his memories of true freedom. Floating in the blackness of space, looking up at the bright, eternal stars, even doing battle with the forces of darkness all felt familiar to him and reminded him of other days, other worlds. Even the silver space suit he perpetually wore (which didn't leave much to the imagination) was reminiscent of the bright, silvery world to which he'd once belonged.

The grass rustled under the thump and creak of his boots. He wished he could take his armor off and really experience the gorgeous night air, but it was not to be, not yet. He had to wear his silver armor all day every day, and the story had not explained why. Roger thought he might be a werewolf. A few recent scenes had shown him hiding from the moon and getting snappish during certain times of the month. He probably wore the silver armor to keep his wolfy side under control. No doubt she'd planned to have him forced to take it off under extreme duress. Then the werewolf would appear and the tension Helene had been talking about would explode.

In what direction was Roger most likely to explode? He wanted badly to have a shot at the Dragon King, but there had been no sign of him since they'd dodged the King's spies a few days before. And there hadn't been a scout or a spy since Diana's arrival that afternoon. Meg called her a goddess, the most powerful witch in the Walled Kingdom or anywhere beyond. Roger didn't know if that was true, but it was true that the Dragon King still hadn't shown his scaly muzzle near here. Maybe he feared that Diana could knock him out of the sky with a glance. Maybe she could.

Roger felt miserably useless. He missed his books. This was not his Book, this odd little adventure he'd been dragged along on. The grass is always greener, he thought with a silent laugh. Once upon a time he'd been bored of traveling through miles of empty space to rescue his perpetually endangered lady love. God, he missed her. She wasn't too bright, but she'd been brave and good-hearted and loyal. A good heart counted for more than a few extra IQ points, in Roger's opinion.

He fancied he could see a silvery speck crossing the darkening heavens. Could that be his ship, looking for him? Sometimes it was sentient, when the plot required it. It once had crossed multiple dimensions to find him, following a tracking device planted in his helmet. Ironically, it was a device his enemies had used to trace and spy on him, but then they'd forgotten to remove it after kidnapping him.

Remembering that made him feel suddenly uneasy and exposed, standing out here in the dark. There were no lights but the stars overhead; the nearest cottages were dark within as their inhabitants slumbered. He should feel secure in the darkness; if he couldn't see, then nobody could see him. But instead he felt naked, as though he were blind and deaf and standing next to a cliff.

Was something watching him right now? Something large and malevolent, staring down through the darkness, watching him with eyes bigger than the night? Roger shivered. He'd had enough fresh air for now.

But the stars were brightening in the night sky, and they were so beautiful to watch. He'd never seen the stars while he was living inside Enchanted Ink. He'd never been able to go outside. He'd tried to follow a customer out into the street once, just to see what would happen, and he'd found himself right back inside the shop, walking into a wall. The only night sky he'd ever seen was inside his Book, and that was a blank, pale sky that faded a little more every year. Whatever magic had brought him into the real world had been slowly dying... until Diana wrote that story about him and brought the magic back. Maybe she really was a goddess.

What would happen to him if that story faded too, and he lost whatever magic was holding him in the real world? Would he fade away into nonexistence, or would he return to whatever world he'd come from? He shivered a bit; he didn't like not knowing what would happen next. In the Book, he always knew. Inside, everything was comfortable and familiar. And in the shop, Helene was always there to protect him and the other characters from the dark things. Here in Diana's world, he had no idea what to expect. He didn't even know who he was. He still thought he might be a werewolf, but he hoped not. In the books he'd read over Helene's shoulder, something always killed the werewolf.

But he couldn't be too angry at Diana. He still remembered the story she'd written for him, about him and Marla. It had made him feel alive and new. Like a real, breathing person. Then Helene had read it aloud, and he'd felt a rush of realness that burst through him and filled the world with color. He owed that feeling to Diana. So if she had decided he needed to come to the Walled Kingdom with Helene, to protect her and the baby Ember, then that was what he would do.

The stars were so bright. Like glowing diamonds, huge and bright. Did the stars in the real world shine like this? Probably not. Helene had commented once that Diana had a knack for taking creative license with reality. She probably thought this brilliant sky was poetic. In reality it was a little frightening.

A few stars vanished. Roger blinked. Was that normal? There was now a small black hole in the middle of the sky. Was it an object hanging there, blocking out the light? It didn't move. Roger blinked again, but the scene didn't change. This seemed odd, but he had no basis for comparison. In his Book there were always black holes and rips in the sky. It was where the monsters came through.

Monsters.

Roger took a deep breath. "Diana!" he shouted.

More stars winked out. "Diana, I need you now!" he called. The backs of his hands felt hot and itchy.

Vellichor

The black rip spread across the sky. A cold breeze blew Roger's face and whistled through his silver armor.

"Diana!" he shouted. Damn it, where was she?

The breeze whistled again, and this time he heard a voice on the wind. It was a woman, and she was screaming.

"Francine?" he asked.

****

Francine scarcely remembered what happened after the Dragon King had seized her in his enormous claws. They had burned her skin like banking coals; she could still feel the scorch marks on her flesh. She thought she remembered Reuben seeing her, calling her name. But it was all a blur, like spinning around and around in a dark room. Now she was free but still spinning, and she couldn't find her way. Every time she thought she was moving in a straight line she stumbled and fell headlong into the blackness. She screamed and caught herself, struggling to her feet—only to feel dizzy and lost again.

How she wished that she had listened to Christopher! But that was how it always went for her. She yearned for male approval, craved it like a drunkard craves wine. But her addiction frustrated her and wounded her image of herself as a strong female character. So she lashed out at the nearest male and did something foolish just to prove that she could. She'd refused to listen to Christopher even though her inner angel had warned her that he was talking sense. She'd walked right into the Dragon King's claws, and she'd probably given the scaly bastard ammunition to use against Reuben. The one man in the universe who she never wanted to hurt.

Where was Reuben now? For that matter, where was the Dragon? She didn't feel his claws on her now, though she could still feel the marks they'd left on her neck and ribs. She'd been stumbling around in the dark for gods knew how long, and it appeared that she was completely alone. It made no sense.

Then, out of nowhere, she heard the gurgling cry of a baby.

Francine stopped moving. The cry was sharp but not unpleasant, and it struck her ears and heart in an odd way. Her breasts prickled, and her nipples sharpened to points. Suddenly she was able to stand upright and look around, not that there was anything to see. She finally recognized this place as the darkness between pages, the place of wild magic that could lead anywhere, and into any story. The cry came again. It wasn't unhappy or frightened. It was the inquisitive chirp of a baby looking for its mother, certain of her presence but unable to see her. It felt familiar to Francine, but she had no idea why. She'd been dead for thirty years and never had a baby, nor even been near one. Not that she could remember.

But all the same, Francine turned slowly in the direction of the cry.

"Francine!"

The voice of Diana, that interfering witch. She'd always disliked her, though she didn't have a concrete reason to. The witch had meant well when she'd tried to lay Francine to rest, back in the shop. She'd had no way of knowing that the boogeyman would grab her. Just one more in a long list of disappointments in Francine's existence.

"It was Francine! Oh my God, how could I have forgotten?"

That was definitely Diana's voice. Francine was alone in the dark, but she felt that human company was very close. Almost too close. She felt smothered.

"What did he do to her? Or did I do it? How could I have forgotten? She never made it into the final draft, and I forgot all about her! I never gave her a chance."

And then, in the dark.

All at once.

She remembered.

She remembered everything.

Francine threw her head back and screamed her fury and grief into the wild, empty darkness.

Her voice ripped a hole in the sky.

Chapter Twenty-One

Apep knew all about Reuben's betrayal as soon as the dragon dust hit the pages of Diana's ultimate weapon. Did the fool think that he could trick a dragon using his own essence? It was disgust at his son's stupidity more than anger at his betrayal that made the Dragon King abandon Francine and leave her to wander alone in the darkness between pages. He washed his claws of them both.

He'd rescued his son from a pointless, perfunctory existence in the mortal world, where he'd wasted years wandering aimlessly and pining after a girl long dead. And this was the thanks he got. Bold-faced betrayal. Reuben hadn't even been subtle about it. It was rude and disrespectful to not at least try.

Apep grumbled and growled to himself as he soared silently through the swirling darkness. For the first time in his existence he had no idea what to do next. He wasn't afraid, just irritated and bewildered. He'd had his takeover of the mortal realm all mapped out and ready to go, but interference from this random cast of characters had thrown him into a tailspin. Now he was at a loss.

He couldn't go back to the Walled Kingdom, not now. Diana was there; she'd mastered the trick of crossing the border between reality and imagination, with a little help from one of the shop's characters. (Some female named Jazzy. Who named a girl that?) Now she was in the world she'd created, and there she was as good as a goddess. If Apep appeared there, she could write him out of existence with a single word. She might even be able to do it now, though she probably didn't know it. So for now he was safe. The darkness between pages was a place of featureless wild magic, and there were no rules here. No rules and no goddesses. He thought he was probably beyond her reach, for now.

He couldn't stay here forever. Nor could he go back to the mortal world. It should be possible now; Helene had acted as some sort of anchor or battery for the spirits that had kept him at bay. Now Helene was gone. It should be wide open as a freeway now.

But if the way was open for him, then it was open for everyone, literally everyone in the Walled Kingdom or any other "fictional" place. Including the boogeyman, the Tentacled Horror, or any number of monsters, wizards, or knights in shining armor. Apep was confident that he was a match for any one opponent. But every opponent ever? Everyone who had ever slain a dragon? He was less confident in his chances there.

What to do, what to do. He should have held on to Francine. He'd dropped her into the darkness in disgust, leaving her to stumble around in the middle of nowhere. Perhaps he'd been too hasty. Diana had forgotten about Francine in the final draft of *Imprisonment of Hope*, but she still had an instinctive fondness for the little nitwit. He might have been able to use her as a bargaining chip, something to buy him enough time to come up with a stronger plan. One that couldn't be shattered by a lot of half-formed story ideas with more guts than sense. Preferably one that involved murdering that sentimental lunatic Helene.

A horrifying shriek ripped through the darkness, knocking Apep out of the air and sending him into a tailspin. Apep bellowed. What the hell was that? He knew who it was; it was his favorite hostage Francine. But why on earth had she screamed like that? It had been more than a verbal cry. She'd somehow tapped into the wild magic of the dark place, and it was coming out in her voice.

Francine screamed again, rending the fabric of the darkness around him. This time Apep was prepared for it, and he only wobbled a little. There was despair in that voice, rage and grief. Francine's heart was shattering. After all she'd been through, all the indignities she'd suffered, she was finally, irrevocably shattered.

That could only mean one thing. At last Diana remembered her. And that meant that Francine remembered. She knew what she'd been and what had been taken from her.

Diana was about to have her hands full. How lovely.

It was time to go back to the Walled Kingdom.

Apep narrowed his eyes and blew out a puff of flame. The wild magic swirled and swam like eddies of smoke in a slow breeze. The Walled Kingdom, he thought fiercely. Open the door, pour the magic in. Fill that land with enough wild magic to burn that witch to a crisp. Then the whole world will be mine.

The Walled Kingdom would be his once again, and he would use the magic there to flood the real world and take control of the ley line crossing. Then the real fun would begin.

Vellichor

Christopher raised his head. "What just happened?" he asked.

The boogeyman flowed past, his robes twitching in agitation. "It's Francine. She's losing her mind."

Christopher listened. Far off, he could hear Francine shrieking. This wasn't unexpected; her lover had just died, after all. But there was a shivery, vibrant quality to the sound that made Christopher think of a sheet flapping in the wind.

"She's losing her mind?" Christopher repeated. "Could you elaborate?"

"No, because I can't actually see what's going on. She's not in the shop. Or—not exactly. All I can tell is that she's having some sort of breakdown, and I only know that because my Lovecraftian influence has given me a nose for insanity."

Christopher looked all around. Nothing to see here but the usual black words and white spaces. "Why can't I see outside the Book like you can?" he said plaintively. "I hate not knowing what's going on."

"I don't think you want to see—oh dear. This is not good."

"Now what? Oh!" Christopher threw his hands out in an attempt to steady himself, but of course there was nothing to touch. Words were real, but they had no substance.

The pages were thinning. The stark whiteness between the thick black words was fading and swirling like mist, and Christopher could see pale grey space beyond. There were shapes out there that he couldn't quite make out, nor did he want to. It was wild magic. He was looking at the darkness between pages.

"What's happening?" Christopher asked. He looked down at his feet, his normal defense when something dark came out of the words. But the pale surface beneath his feet was also swirling, shifting, sliding away like a white curtain. "What's going on? What did you do?"

"I didn't do anything." The boogeyman's normally wry voice was thin and shaken.

The boogeyman was afraid? Christopher's heart went cold, and his throat seemed to close. The boogeyman was the embodiment of fear itself. What on earth could make him afraid?

Nothing on earth, obviously. Christopher listened, and it seemed that Francine's voice was getting louder. She wasn't just screaming now; she was shrieking, cursing, and sobbing. Whatever breakdown was suffering, it was affecting the fabric that separated the real world from the Book.

"We have to go back to the shop," he said. "We need to see what's going on out there."

"What good will that do?" The boogeyman's laconic tone was back.

"I might be able to help!"

"Without Helene? She's the source of your existence. How can you have any agency without her to guide you?"

Christopher glared. "Because she's a good fucking writer!"

The boogeyman recoiled. "Well. Perhaps you're right."

He reached out with a black, withered finger and touched Christopher's chest. Something inside popped, like a dislocated joint snapping back into place. A cold ache that Christopher had barely been aware of disappeared, and he took a deep, cleansing breath.

"You're free," the boogeyman said. Was there a note of affection in the old ghoul's voice? "Go change the story."

Christopher looked back, at the swirling, darkening mist. "I'm free," he said with a fierce grin. And he leapt into the mist.

****

The boogeyman watched Christopher disappear into the gathering darkness and felt nothing but relief. He'd captured the lad as a lark, an homage to the dark faerie he'd once been before being lured in by the Book. And for a long time it had been a treat to feed on the boy's fear and taunt his creator. But now everything was so different. The Dragon King was still out there, and his creator seemed to have no idea how to control him. The shop, always a crossing point for creatures on both sides of the veil, was now becoming a morass, a traffic jam. The right blow at the wrong time could destroy everything.

And now—the boogeyman listened with dawning dread—Francine was complicating matters further. The boogeyman barely understood what was going on outside his Book, but two things he knew all about were fear and madness. Right now he was listening to a combination of both.

He stared at the swirling, misty pages. It was all completely porous now; instead of a small rip or hole, anyone could just step from one world to the next without preamble. The boogeyman had no interest in exploring other worlds or other books. He was happy enough right here, in his own space where fear ruled. Antagonists like the Dragon King had never made sense to him. He'd successfully conquered the Walled Kingdom, so why push it farther? Why risk everything in a mad grab for power in a world he'd never be a part of?

The boogeyman didn't want to leave his Book at all; he didn't even want to go back to the shop at the moment. There was a fire in the shop, and what would become of him if his Book was burned up while he was on the other side of it? All the same, he was curious about what was going on elsewhere. Where was Christopher now? Had he made it back to the shop, or had this horrible thinness confused and disoriented him? The boogeyman no longer had any power over him, but as characters from the same story he did have an awareness that he could use to track the boy's movements. He focused now, looking for that silvery tether that bound him and Christopher together.

He had made it back to the shop, the boogeyman discovered. The fire had taken over much of the back office, but the main book shop was mostly untouched except for a bit of smoke. The boogeyman shivered. What would fire do to book characters? Would they feel the flames? Would they experience true death, or would they just go back to the faerie world they'd come from? He didn't want to think about it. At least the fire was well away from Sci Fi, Fantasy, and Horror. For now.

Christopher was wandering around the shop like he'd never been there before. What was he thinking? The shop was closed and empty of life.

The only life was crackling away in the office. If Christopher wanted to be helpful, he should be looking for a way to bring the real people, Helene and Diana, back so they could put out the fire or call 911 or whatever real people did in such situations.

The boy was at the front register, where *Imprisonment of Hope* still lay. A pity it wasn't closer to the fire, though it had proven remarkably fire-resistant in the past. Christopher was staring at the goddam book like he'd never seen it before. What was he thinking of?

Normally characters couldn't touch real books. Couldn't pick them up, couldn't read them, couldn't flip the pages. But Christopher didn't always follow the rules, possibly because his creator kept forgetting he wasn't real. The antipsychotics helped, but they weren't a cure.

And—yes. Here he was, picking the damn thing up and flipping the pages like he had the right. What was he doing? The boogeyman felt a prickle of frustration. If he hadn't freed the kid, he could read his mind right now and find out.

****

Diana heard Roger's shout and handed Ember to Meg. "I'd better see what that's about," she said. "The Dragon King might be trying to pull something."

"He shouldn't be able to do anything without you knowing," Jazzy said. She got up and followed Diana out the door. "Aren't you the writer?"

"I don't know anything at all about this kind of magic," Diana sighed. "None of the books I've read—"

She got outside and froze when she saw what Roger was staring at. As she'd once envisioned, the sky was punctured by stars: a blue-black curtain stabbed and slashed by stark white clusters of brightness. But just above the horizon was a wide swath of blackness where no stars twinkled. A cold breeze chilled her face. It smelled like dust and old paper.

Faintly, on the breeze, she heard a woman screaming.

"Francine," Helene whispered. Diana hadn't even known she'd followed them out here. "That's Francine's voice."

"What's going on?" Jazzy's voice was cold and calm, but when Diana glanced at her she saw the younger woman's face was pale as milk.

"Apep!" Diana shouted. "I know you're out there! Show yourself! Apep! I speak your true name!"

No answer. Just that weird black swath, the cold breeze, and Francine's wailing cry. Wherever she was, she sounded like she'd lost her mind. Diana's heart surged with fear and guilt. What was the Dragon King doing to her now?

She said Apep's true name two more times, but there was still no response. If he was in the Walled Kingdom, he would have to answer her. She was in his world and knew his true name; she should be able to own him.

But he knew better than to appear here. He was hiding in the darkness between pages, safely out of sight. He'd ripped a hole in the world, but he wasn't doing anything with it. What was that bastard up to?

****

Vellichor

Apep lurked on the other side of the tear. He heard Diana say his true name, but since he was in neither the Walled Kingdom nor the real world, he was able to resist its pull. Any moment now some heroic fool was going to venture too close to the tear, and then he would have a handy hostage. He wondered what it would be like to kill his creator. He hoped to have the chance to find out, though he'd settle for the baby.

Francine was crying, sobbing like a madwoman, and her voice was getting closer. Bless her heart, she always showed up when he needed her. He flexed his claws. Maybe he could charm her over to his side as he had Reuben. She had plenty of reason to be pissed off at Diana, and anger was his weapon of choice.

Francine's voice was getting closer. Any moment now.

****

Helene felt frozen in place. She barely knew whether to inhale or exhale. She hadn't felt this confused and blocked since Christopher had been captured by the boogeyman.

She turned back toward the cottage, where Meg still held baby Ember. Then she looked at Diana, Roger, and the enormous rip in the sky. Francine's mindless scream had given way to sobs and curses. The air felt thick and fraught, and the smell of old books filled her nose.

"What's going on?" Jazzy cried. "What are we supposed to do?"

They all looked at Diana, who shook her head slowly. "I don't know," she said faintly.

"I don't know what happens next."

Dawn Napier

Chapter Twenty-Two

Francine's breath came hot and fast. She felt as though she'd been set on fire from the inside out. Her lungs burned, and her heart was a molten lump. Now she really knew what heartbreak was. It wasn't sadness or depression or that petty loneliness that had once governed her days. It was this hot, burning horror that scalded her soul and made her feel like a living funeral pyre. She wasn't just broken. She was burned alive.

Diana had written her out of her own book and forgotten her. Her child had been taken from her and handed over to someone else. Her love, her Reuben, her precious daughter's father, had been taken from her. She'd lost everything, all because that word-witch hadn't cared for her character.

Diana was about to get a lesson in what made a strong female character.

****

The Dragon King hissed in satisfaction. Yes! Francine's rage was consuming her, and she was ready to burn it all down just to get at Diana and teach her a lesson. Perfect. Time to reel the fish into the boat.

He didn't know quite where she was, but he didn't expect that to pose a problem. Mindless rage was his element, and he could still hear Francine crying hers out into the universe. All he had to do was follow his nose, so to speak.

Oh Francine, he thought as he flew, at last you have a reason for existing. How proud you must be. Come, my girl. We'll get that writer bitch together.

YES.

Apep froze in midair as something huge seized him by the mind and spoke directly into his reptilian brain. One wing caught on something in the darkness, and he heard a painful crack.

"Francine?" he hissed cautiously. "Is that you? How strong you have become!"

One wing flapped uselessly; the other hung limp. It didn't hurt, not yet. Here in the darkness between pages he wasn't quite corporeal and didn't feel pain. But he'd feel it plenty when he got back to the Walled Kingdom.

YES. There was no anger or fear in the word. Only a cold statement of fact.

YOU KILLED REUBEN.

"I didn't!" Apep hated the whiny, reptilian tone in his own voice. "I set him free! That tentacled thing ate him!"

YOU DROPPED ME INTO THE DARKNESS TO DIE. AND YOU ABANDONED REUBEN. NOW YOU'RE TRYING TO KILL OUR CHILD.

Shit. She was thinking more clearly than she had any right to, in her mad grief. Francine—or whatever she'd become—had a grip on this throat that was tightening. It still didn't hurt, but something else was happening. He felt weak and tired. Almost calm. Apep was never calm. He was always angry, and anger was the source of his power.

Francine's lips tickled his ear. Her breath was warm and moist. Apep smelled old books. "You killed my man, and now you want to destroy my home. My child."

Apep had never felt fear before. He thought he was dying. Maybe he was. His good wing flapped helplessly. He lashed out with his claws, but they felt only air. Francine had him in a death grip by the neck, but he couldn't touch her. What was she?

He didn't know. And it terrified him, even more than the ever-tightening noose.

****

The shop was dark and empty, except for the flickering fire in the office. Christopher shoved a pile of dusty old books out of the way and shut the ancient door. It creaked like a dying crow, and Christopher had to slam it several times to get it to latch. Thankfully the fire hadn't spread far. How much time had passed since Reuben had dropped the dragon dust all over Diana's manuscript? He had no idea. Brach's body was almost invisible among the flames, but he didn't know how long it would take a body to burn. They were mostly water, so would it even burn at all? It didn't matter. He'd never been clear on how time worked among the different realities that converged here in Enchanted Ink.

He walked around the shop, stepping as carefully as a tightrope walker. He was aware of every sensation, every scent and sound and even taste. The cheap carpet was rough and nubbly under his feet. The omnipresent scent of old books mingled with the smell of burning paper. It smelled a bit like weed smoke. How would he know what weed smelled like? Because Helene knew. Funny how that worked.

Behind the crackling of the fire in the office, he could still hear Francine. Her shrieks had given way to heartbroken sobs. She sounded like Helene's mother had cried in the weeks after her miscarriage. Helene had been nine, and her mom had tried to keep her mourning private. It hadn't worked; her sobs had woken Helene up every night for almost a month.

Christopher didn't know what had happened to Francine to make her cry like this, but his heart ached for her nevertheless. Nobody deserved to feel that kind of pain.

He stopped at the front desk, where Helene had spent so many hours chatting with customers and cataloguing books. He missed her so much. He had never cried before—not that he could remember—but if he could cry for Helene, it might sound like Francine.

The swirling grey mist was in here too, he noticed. He wasn't surprised. Enchanted Ink had always been a thin spot in reality, and all the crossing back and forth, characters hopping into each other's Books… the fabric was bound to come apart eventually. Christopher could probably step into any book he chose right now.

Maybe he could go to the Walled Kingdom. Maybe he could go find Helene.

But—he glanced back at the office, where smoke was billowing under the door. The manuscript was long gone. Whatever protective magic had kept it free of the flames had died with Reuben. There was probably a way to cross over without the physical book, but Christopher didn't want to risk getting lost in the dark.

Vellichor

Sitting on the desk next to the computer was *Imprisonment of Hope*, that goddam book that had started all this. Maybe there was a safer way to get there.

He stroked the cover, then picked it up. One of the upsides to being a character with a schizophrenic writer was that he wasn't always subject to the rules of being fictional. He'd always been the only character who could read any book he wanted. Funny that he'd never really thought about it, or wondered why it was so.

He opened the book to the last page. Baby Ember, the newly born Chosen One, lay snug in a basket while her guardians discussed her fate. In this book they were nameless, unidentified. In the next, they would be known as Helene and Roger.

Helene, he thought with feeling. I miss you so much.

He hugged the book to his chest, where his heart pounded painfully. Helene. My heart. I miss you. I want to be with you again, in any world.

The swirling grey mist darkened, and a cool breeze teased his beard. Christopher closed his eyes and thought, as hard as he could, Helene.

When he opened his eyes, the shop was gone. He was outside, standing in a grassy expanse under a ceiling of painfully bright stars.

"Where am I now?" he asked, barely daring to hope.

"Christopher!"

His heart thudded louder. Could it be? He shut his eyes again, not wanting to get too excited. The book dropped from his tingling fingers.

Seconds later, a familiar body slammed into his, wrapping him in a trembling embrace. Curly hair tickled his nose. It smelled like old books.

"Helene," he whispered, and for a moment the entire universe faded from his awareness.

When they broke, Christopher looked around sheepishly, ready to apologize for the PDA. But nobody was looking at them at all. Diana, Jazzy, and Roger all stood in a loose group, staring up at the impossibly bright sky.

Helene looked up as well. "It's getting bigger," she murmured.

There was a gap of blackness in the sea of stars. "What is it?" he asked.

"We don't know." Helene shivered and snuggled against his chest. "I've missed being able to do this."

Her body was warm against his, and he closed his eyes briefly. Then he opened them again. Focus, he told himself. We don't have time for a reunion.

A violent roar split the sky and trembled the earth. Helene screamed, and Diana shouted a curse.

"What's happening?" Roger demanded.

"It's the Dragon King," Diana said. "Francine is killing him. No. She's using him. Feeding on him. She's going to tear the world apart."

"If she's killing the dragon, isn't that a good thing?"

Diana shook her head wildly. Her think grey hair made a pale halo around her face. "I didn't write this!" she wailed. "This is not how the story was supposed to go! And—" she shuddered. "—I don't know what will happen." She finished in a weak whine.

Then she said it again, more forcefully. "I don't know what will happen."

"Is that why there's a hole in the sky?" Jazzy asked. Her voice was thin and fearful. "Because you don't know what happens next?"

"Probably." Diana paused, listening to the wind. "But I don't know!" she burst out. She sounded near tears.

The Dragon King roared again, but it was weak and ended with a hacking cough. Diana moaned.

"Francine's absorbing the Dragon King. She's—eating—his rage." Roger looked all around and spoke rapidly. "Does anyone else hear that?"

Christopher heard a lot of things. He heard Francine crying and cursing, the dragon bellowing, and very faintly, Helene whimpering against his chest. But now there was something new. A flapping sound, like a sheet of paper in the breeze.

A lot of sheets of paper in a very heavy breeze.

"Oh shit," Christopher breathed. "Now what?"

****

Now what? Helene wondered as she clung to Christopher's chest. She was aware that she looked like a helpless blonde damsel clinging to her hero, but she didn't care it felt good to finally hold him again.

But now something else was coming, as though they didn't have enough problems.

She peeped round Christopher's shoulder to see the others staring up at the sky again. More crazy shit coming out of the sky. Of course.

Roger, she saw, was unbuckling his armor. How strange. Earlier in the story he'd said it was forbidden for him to remove it in any way. And if they were in for a fight, now would not be the time to take off his protection, would it?

Helene looked up slowly to see what had drawn the others' gaze. The sky was full of dragons.

Real dragons. Not harpies, not wyverns, not the tree lizards with flattened tails that allowed them to drift from tree to tree. Dragons. At least six of them, maybe as many as ten. They were a series of streaming, flapping shapes against the backdrop of stars. Still far away, but coming closer.

Real dragons, from outside the Walled Kingdom. The people here had built those walls to protect themselves from external threats. Nothing on two or four legs could get in or out.

But creatures with wings—oh that was a different can of worms altogether, wasn't it?

It was more than twelve dragons. They were still coming. The Walled Kingdom was no longer a sanctuary. Now it was a food bowl for monsters.

"Look," Roger said. "The full moon is rising."

****

The moon was huge, rising into the darkness like a glaring eye. Roger's breath was harsh and fast, his heart thudding in his throat. His eyes burned as though he were feverish. His mouth felt dry, and his teeth itched.

His armor was too tight. It pressed on his body, cutting off his strength. Slowly he removed a gauntlet and let it fall to the ground. The cool air felt wonderful on his furry hand. He pulled off the other gauntlet.

"Roger," Diana said in a low voice.

"It's okay," he said distantly. He felt as though he were speaking from outside his body. He was hot

244

all over. He took off his helm. "It's okay. I can do this."

"I can't save you, Roger. Not from here."

"I know. Tell Marla I love her."

His heart pounded so hard he fancied he could hear it thudding against his breastplate. He unbuckled his shoulder straps, loosening it. One of the buckles jammed, and with a casual tug he snapped it in two. The padding underneath was soaked with sweat.

The first of the dragons circled lower, preparing to land. Roger bared his teeth, ready to die for his pack.

****

Helene slowly drew away from Christopher. She felt like she had to do something, but she had no idea what. Diana was completely frozen, locked in place like a stalled-out robot. Francine somehow had a hold of the Dragon King, and he seemed to be dying. Perhaps his dying roars had summoned the other dragons from beyond the Walled Kingdom, or perhaps they were attracted to the rip in the sky. But they were here for whatever reason, and they were getting closer. Roger had shed the last of his armor and now stood on all fours, ears and fangs bristling. And Jazzy... was staring down at the ground. Helene followed her gaze and saw *Imprisonment of Hope*, that last unbeatable copy that had haunted her shop for days. It lay in the grass next to Helene's feet where Christopher had dropped it.

Her face and hands felt numb as she bent down to pick it up. She hadn't touched the book in days, not since Diana had plucked it out of her hands. It had sat on the front desk, ignored by every customer that passed by.

Helene was terrified to touch it now. This book had almost allowed the Dragon King, a monster of perfect rage, to slide over into the real world. She'd come so close to the end. There was only one sentence left.

Only one sentence left.

Helene ran her fingers over the cover. Nice sturdy hardcover, in excellent condition despite missing the dust jacket. There had only been five hundred of these printed. The publisher had been a small press, both unwilling and unable to invest hugely in an unknown author of dubious literary pedigree.

Helene opened the book and flipped through a few yellow-tinged pages. On every page, over and over in bold letters, were the words HELP ME HELP ME HELP ME.

Why should I? Helene thought fiercely. You've done nothing but hurt and kill people ever since Diana thought of you. For the last fifty pages you've been trying to kill a baby, for fuck's sake.

THERE IS NO HOPE WITHOUT ADVERSITY. IF I DIE HOPE DIES.

Helene glanced up at the circling dragons. It sounded like a fortune cookie platitude, but could it be true? Did the future of the Walled Kingdom depend on the fate of that horrible beast?

Or was he talking about a different sort of hope: a child whose name meant Hope?

What the hell. What did they have to lose?

She'd soon find out.

Vellichor

The first dragon landed on a low hill and came galloping at them before its wings were folded. Roger howled a challenge and raced to meet it. Jazzy tried to follow, pathetically slow on her two human legs.

Helene flipped to the last page. To the last sentence of the last page.

"And as the baby gurgled up at the spinning toy, the young peasant woman thought that was the most magical sound in the world.

"Hope, she thought, lived on in the voice of every child."

Helene closed the book with a dusty thump.

"The end!" she shouted.

Chapter Twenty-Three

The hair-ruffling breeze became a gale, and the smell of old books flooded the air. The book in Helene's hands blackened like burning paper and crumbled into sparking black dust.

Francine's cries cut off like a light switch, and a blast of yellow-white fire blasted through the hole in the sky.

"He's coming," Christopher whispered. "Whatever you did, it freed him from Francine."

What had happened to Francine, though? No time to wonder about that now. More dragons were landing and galloping towards them. Roger, now shaped like a wolf the size of a small deer, was charging at the leader with his ears and tail up. Jazzy loped after him, straggling behind like a forgotten child.

The dragons paused in their approach and glanced up at the rip in the sky. The flames died, and a winged black shape appeared against the backdrop of stars.

The Dragon King was returning to the Walled Kingdom at last.

He landed in a grassy expanse between the humans and the dragons. He hissed at the approaching dragons, and they raised their heads as though in surprise. The dragon in the lead—Helene thought it might be green, though it was hard to tell in the dim starlight—lowered its head and hissed at Roger, who bristled and circled him on stiff legs.

Vellichor

The Dragon King slinked up to Diana and cocked his enormous head. He blinked his golden eyes and grinned at her toothily.

Christopher tried to grab Helene, but she shook him off and ran to her friend's side. Diana never took her eyes off the enormous beast.

"I can't kill you, can I?" she said.

The Dragon King blinked and became a handsome older man in black robes. "No, my love," he said with a sad smile. "No more than you can kill the stars."

Diana's head snapped to the side. "Roger?" she said. "You and Jazzy go check on Francine."

Roger stood up, his fangs and fur disappearing like mist. Jazzy finally caught up with him and took his hand, and a moment later they were both gone.

Diana turned back to the Dragon King. "What can I do?" she whispered. "I don't know what happens next."

The King grinned. "How does it feel to be mortal like the rest of us for once?"

"Don't you mock me," Diana said fiercely.

"I wasn't mocking. It's the truth. I don't know what happens next either. Nobody does."

They stared at each other in the silent darkness. Then a voice came from the night behind them. "Perhaps we can help."

Meg walked out of the cottage, her rippling red hair hair glowing with its own inner light. In her arms, Baby Ember clapped and waved her fat little arms.

"Ember," Helene whispered. "Hope."

****

The darkness between pages was like a black snowstorm. Cold wind swirled all around, and something sharp stung Roger's face like tiny needles.

"What's going on?" Jazzy clung to Roger's arm. "It's not usually like this!"

"It's Francine. She's doing something."

"How do we make it stop?"

Roger turned around in a slow circle. The cold wind swirled around them like a twister, but it seemed colder and harsher from one direction. "We have to find her first," he said. "Come on." He took her hand, and together they pressed forward, into the black storm.

Thinly they heard her voice. "You stay away from me! Leave me alone!"

"Francine we want to help you," Jazzy called. "Please let us in!"

"Nobody can help me…" Her voice was fading, as though she was moving away down a dark hallway.

"Yes, we can!" Jazzy's voice was deep and urgent. "Just let us in! Please."

"She took my baby away. I'm all alone now."

Jazzy sighed. "I know. We know what happened to you. You were forgotten and lied to. But please, it's not over. It doesn't have to be over for you."

The cold wind buffeted Roger's face. He lowered his head and tried to press forward, but he had the sensation of being pushed backwards, away from whatever magical cataclysm Francine's misery had conjured.

"It is over. I'm dead. The book's been written, and Helene read every word. I'll be alone forever."

"Help me get to her," Jazzy whispered. "We need to make her understand."

"I'm trying," Roger said through gritted teeth. His cheeks and ears were numb from the cold.

"Not like that, you square. Brute strength doesn't work here. Feel for her. Try to reach her with your mind."

Roger had no idea how to do that. His character arc was based on strength, with a little cleverness and laser power thrown in when needed. But he tried. He thought about Marla, how alone he would feel if she died and he had no way to save her.

His heart went cold. What a horrifying thought. His whole reason for living was to love and protect her. He had little agency beyond protection of the women in his life, Helene and Diana as well as Marla.

Was that what Francine felt now, with Reuben gone and her baby in danger? His throat closed, and he sniffed deeply. How terrible.

"Yes," Jazzy whispered. The cold wind died, and they were in a dark, silent room. Curled up in a heap in front of them was a vague female shape who could only be Francine.

****

Meg walked up to the Dragon King with a brilliant smile. "Hello, sweetie," she said.

He blinked. "I thought you were dead."

"Chastity died years ago, when you stole her son and twisted his heart. I'm Meg. And this is your grandchild."

"The one prophesied to defeat rage," he whispered. There was a strange note in his voice, some new strength. Helene edged back away from Diana.

"At last, the chosen one is within my reach. Thank you, witch, for delivering her to me." The robed man became a dragon again, and a gout of white-hot fire erupted from his maw. It engulfed the woman and child. Christopher ran forward and grabbed Helene, throwing her to the ground. Diana screamed.

When the flames died, baby Ember laughed and clapped her chubby hands. Meg smiled. "You can't kill a dragon child with fire, you fool."

The Dragon King growled and snapped at the infant with his toothy jaws. The baby laughed again.

"You can't kill her like that either." Meg shook her glowing hair, sending sparks drifting to the ground.

The dragon became a man, and he reached for the baby with gnarled old hands. "Then I'll kill her with a man's hands," he snarled. He grabbed the baby's neck, but again the child just laughed. She patted his scrawny arm and said, "Papa."

The Dragon King withdrew. Helene got to her feet and whispered, "What's going on?"

Meg glanced back at her briefly. Then she turned back to the Dragon King. "You can't kill hope, darling. Not like this. Not with brute strength."

Diana smiled. Helene leaned over and whispered, "Don't you think the symbolism is a bit heavy-handed?"

"If it means we get to go home, I'll take it," Diana said. "I can always tweak it on the re-write."

Vellichor

One of the other dragons approached. Helene tensed, but he never looked at them. He nudged the Dragon King, who shifted back to dragon form and lowered his enormous head.

"It's over," the other dragon rumbled. "It's time to go home."

The Dragon King, a king no longer, followed his brothers over the hill. The large green beast turned back and said to the humans, "This kingdom has too many walls."

Diana smiled a little. "I agree."

One by one the dragons disappeared into the darkness. Diana couldn't hear it yet, but she could picture it in her mind: the series of heavy crashes that would ripple through the air like violent storms. Dust would fly, and the sky would darken at the nation's borders. Peasants would cower in their beds, and witches would mutter charms to protect them from the wrath of the gods.

But the dragons would not commit acts of wrath in this story. They were acts of mercy.

"Time to go home," Diana repeated. She took Helene and Christopher's hands in hers, and the three of them looked up at the rip in the sky, a tear that was now starting to close.

Helene closed her eyes and breathed deeply of the cool, fresh air that smelled like old books. *Hope,* she thought.

****

Jazzy hunkered down and touched Francine's shoulder. "Come back to the shop with us," she said.

"Why?" Francine's voice was muffled. "Everyone there hates me. I can't do anything. All I know is Reuben, and he's gone."

Jazzy gathered the girl's limp form into her arms. "Because there's still hope," she said. "You're still here. You're still here. Your soul still exists, even though you think there's nothing left to live for. And Reuben didn't die, you know. Just his character. His soul still exists, too. And I think he'll find his way back to you."

"What do you mean?" Francine lifted her head and looked at Jazzy, then at Roger. "*Imprisonment of Hope* was destroyed. He can't ever come back to the shop."

"You don't remember," Roger said. He stepped forward and put his hand on her shoulder. "I don't blame you; your character has been through a lot. But there was another world once, a misty world full of magic and faeries. Do you remember?"

Francine blinked. She looked up into the endless night of the darkness between pages, and for a moment Roger thought he saw a glimmer of understanding in her dark eyes. Then she shook her head. "No."

Jazzy rose to her feet, bringing Francine with her. "Just come back to the shop. Talk to some of the other characters. They remember. They'll tell you."

Too tired to fight further, Francine allowed herself to be led back home. To the world between worlds.

****

The fire department was only two blocks away from Enchanted Ink, so they were able to get the blaze under control before it spread very far beyond the office where it had started. The discovery of Brach's body made it a homicide investigation, but the police thought that a homeless man had simply wandered in and started it by accident, possibly with a bottle of booze or a lit cigarette. It was a mystery why the overhead sprinklers never went off, since the fire marshal had just tested everything the week before and found it in perfect order. But aside from the burned out office and some water damage from the hoses, most of the shop was still intact when Helene and Diana walked in the front door a few minutes later.

Helene watched the stretcher roll out the front door and shook her head. "I can't believe he's gone," she said. Uncle Brach had been an inconstant friend, but someone she could always count on to show up sooner or later. It felt weird to think that he was never going to wander randomly into her life again.

Diana tapped Helene's forehead. "That's because he's not," she said. "People are like stories. Even after you finish reading, the story stays with you. Even if the book burns." Diana's voice hitched a little, and Helene threw her arms around the older woman. Diana hugged her back fiercely. "He would want us to have a happy ending," Helene whispered. They stood there like that for several minutes, until a polite cough from the police chief pulled them apart.

Diana talked to the fire chief, Greg, while Helene called her insurance agent. "So the shop was closed when the fire started," Greg said. "In the middle of a Friday?"

"A friend of ours was having man trouble," Diana said casually. "We closed up for a while to go talk to her."

"Both of you went?"

Diana cocked her head. "Are you implying something?"

Greg shrugged. "No. We're pretty sure the John Doe started the fire somehow, though we're not sure how. There's no sign of an accelerant or explosive, so it probably wasn't deliberate vandalism. Maybe he dropped a lit cigarette on a stack of papers, or there was some kind of electrical malfunction with that old-ass typewriter. Who was he, anyway? Did you know him?"

"I did." Diana looked down at her shoes. "We were old friends, a long time ago."

"Did he have any other friends or family in the area? Someone we need to contact about this?"

Diana shook her head silently. Greg saw her expression and changed the subject.

"So does Helene have a roommate or a boyfriend around? I want to recommend that you guys stay somewhere else while the office is being rebuilt. You never know when something's been weakened by the fire and could collapse."

"No, she's always lived alone, except when I'm crashing with her." Diana looked around the shop. Underneath the smell of old smoke and metal water she could still smell old books. That magic smell.

"Odd. Brian over there said he saw someone heading up the stairs to her apartment while we were checking the smoke detectors. Young guy, scruffy hair?"

Diana shrugged. "Maybe the shop is haunted."

Greg laughed. "Well that would explain why Brian also thought he saw Sherlock Holmes high-fiving a teddy bear in the back earlier. I think he forgot to put on his mask and breathed too much smoke."

Vellichor

Diana laughed with him. "He should write that down. It would make a great story."

Epilogue

The fairy mist sparkled under the brilliant sun, and the sprites that lived and played there chased each other happily in and out of the shadows. Some shadows were pale grey; others were black as pitch. The sprites for the most part avoided the black shadows, which they believed led to dark places filled with dark things.

One sprite, though, was bolder than the others. He moved among the shadows, drawing closer, peering into the dark, then darting away. His golden wings fluttered nervously, every instinct warning him to go back to the top of the mist, where the sun was warm and the sky was safe.

But he couldn't stay away. A vague loneliness tugged at his heart, as though he missed someone he had forgotten. Over and over he returned to the shadows, searching for he knew not what.

Eventually he knew that he would find what he was looking for. These dark shadows were not things but doorways, leading to other worlds. In one of those worlds was a love so deep it transcended life and eternity. He knew she was waiting for him, and he would find her. Eventually he would find the shadow that would take him back home.

The sprites of the fairy realm were eternal. He could search for as long as it took.

About the Author

Dawn Napier grew up in Waukegan IL, and upstate New York. She has a husband, three children, and a ridiculous number of pets. She grew up reading Stephen King, Isaac Asimov, Mercedes Lackey, and Piers Anthony. When she's not reading and writing, she is hiking with her dogs, napping with her cat, or cleaning up after her herd of adopted guinea pigs.

Visit her online on Facebook and her website dawnsdarktreasures.com!

www.ingramcontent.com/pod-product-compliance
Lightning Source LLC
Chambersburg PA
CBHW030243200626
46816CB00002BA/489